Alaskans

Also by Tanyo Ravicz

Ring of Fire and Other Stories
A Man of His Village
Ring of Fire

Alaskans

Stories

———

Tanyo Ravicz

Denali Press

Alaskans
Stories

Copyright © 2014 by Tanyo Ravicz

Published by Denali Press

ISBN: 978-0-9961054-3-9
ISBN (mobi): 978-0-9961054-4-6
ISBN (epub): 978-0-9961054-5-3
Library of Congress Control Number: 2014908946
Denali Press, Palm Springs, CA

First Denali Press Edition
www.denalibooks.com
Inquiries: denalipress@denalibooks.com
Denali Press logo is a trademark of Denali Press.

Nine of these stories were previously published in slightly different form in *Bellowing Ark, The Iconoclast, Frontiers,* and *Conte.* Copyright © 1996, 1997, 2000, 2002, 2003, 2004, 2007 by Tanyo Ravicz. Grateful acknowledgment is made to the editors of these magazines.

These are works of fiction.

Martina

Contents

Author's Note

My pianist friend tells me that she begins her concerts with a short piece to warm up the ears of her audience. This preface is meant to be my short piece. Readers may find a natural progression in the stories as they are arranged in this book, but some may choose to skip around. I like this arrangement of the stories because it gives me a sweeping sense of my own years in Alaska. It also roughly correlates with the order in which the stories were written, but only roughly, and a reader could with justice begin with "Of Knives and Men," which is the narrative of a tenderfoot.

The last three stories in the book are the most recent. I did them in California after I had moved from Alaska. The other stories were written over the course of the previous decade. The market for short fiction is abysmal and I am indebted to the editors who saw fit to publish my work in their pages.

"A Fox in May" stands a little apart from the others in length and manner. Every story has a form and voice that emerge naturally from the author's efforts to make something of a certain subject. This happens to be the last story I composed in longhand: I was living in the bush at the time and had nothing else to write with but a pen.

"One Less Black Bear" is one of the short stories that got me admitted to the writing program at U.C. Irvine in the 1990s. I dropped out of the program after three months and went back to Alaska. The story was published in a little magazine in Texas called *Frontiers* which is now defunct, a fate that isn't unusual in the shoestring world of literary magazines.

In Tahoe I once had the pleasure of sitting in on a discussion of "Fishes and Wine." My story was attacked for being politically correct and again for being politically incorrect. I guess it had to be one or the other. A pox, an incurable pox, on both their houses.

There is always a story that kicks around for years and never gets published even though the editors keep writing you little notes saying it is unique and they are sure you will have no trouble getting it published. In this collection, "Robbie Fox" is that story.

The upside to not getting your writing easily published is that you will keep making it better. In a sense, all our words are written in water. But in another sense we should be carving our sentences in stone.

Tanyo Ravicz
Palm Springs, California
January 2008

Alaskans

A Fox in May

1

The chickens had begun to disappear, one after another, and to tell the truth nobody took much notice at first. So many other concerns weighed on the Hanson family, a chicken's disappearance competed poorly for their attention. But when two of his flock went missing on a single moonless night in May, Jed Hanson, certain in the morning that he hadn't miscounted them, turned from the coop crushing his hands to the sides of his face and ran to the house yelling for his grandfather.

"It's Blind Boy," he cried. "Blind Boy's gone!"

Grandpa Henry, outfitted with his newfangled hearing aids, heard Jed at once and came out on the porch to meet him, Jed racing up the yard at full tilt, the white sleeves of his school shirt rippling in the chilly morning air.

"It's got to be a fox," he panted, "it's got to be."

"Think so?" Old Henry shut the door to keep the mosquitos out.

"I should have locked them in the coop last night."

"It isn't your fault, Jed."

"Oh, I don't know..." Jed knotted his hands together, feeling hot in the face and confused. What had become of his favorite Cornish Cross? Poor Blind Boy! "Don't let them out of the run today, Grandpa. I'm going to lock them in the coop tonight. I wish I didn't have to go. Will you watch them for me? Will you?"

Jed had his grandfather's assurances that he would, but even so, all day at school he thought of nothing but his lost chickens. The mystery of their disappearance preoccupied him and his morning panic kept him restless in class after class.

What made it worse, there was nobody at school he could confide in. At the age of thirteen Jed was bound to nourish more in private than public his tender attachment to his flock. His eighth-grade friends, those who knew of his chickens and had asked to be allowed to view their (when the awful time came) slaughter, would have understood the antagonism Jed was now thrown into: *A thief is making off with Jed Hanson's chickens.* But could the same boys appreciate how soft and fragile the chicks had felt in his hands on the day he first held them at the feed store? How piteously they had twittered in the back seat during the drive home, how sweetly they tipped their beaks up to drink their first sugar water?

And the guilt that he suffered, especially on behalf of the defenseless, one-eyed chicken named Blind

Boy, could he have explained this to anybody without blushing? Or the gloomy futility that overcame him at his desk when he shut his eyes and leaned his head in his hands and, in spite of himself, imagined the violent deaths as they had likely occurred on the night before while he himself slept soundly in his bed?

It was quite possible that the red fox they had seen at the beginning of May had in fact been reconnoitering the chicken run. Not that he actually stopped and leered at the birds, nothing so obvious. "He knows they're there, he can smell them," Grandpa had said.

This happened in broad daylight. Willoughby, Jed's sister, was with them at the time, watching from the picture window as the fox, red-maned, his white-tipped tail bobbing in a leisurely fashion, trotted past the garage and chicken coop without once actually looking at the coop.

The fox crossed the Hanson yard and struck uphill into the dense and drab tangles of leafless willow and wild rose that proliferated beyond the family's woodpile. Hardly a second passed before the fox came rocketing out of the willows in the opposite direction. He plunged down the hill, entered the woods beyond the Hanson garage, and in the blink of an eye had emerged on the dirt road fronting their property. And now they saw the reason for the wild turn in the fox's manner: just out of reach, not three inches above his straining mouth, a plump grouse was flying.

The fox and grouse disappeared together in the woods on the far side of the road. Jed and his sister and his grandfather broke into laughter, moved by something comical in what they had seen. They speculated as to the fate of the pair, now in favor of the fox and now of the grouse, but there was no telling if the fox ever caught the grouse or if this was a case of the fox being outfoxed and his hunger catching him out first.

After school Jed strolled downtown to the Key Bank building and met his mother at the law offices where she was employed as a paralegal secretary. The day was Friday, the spring break-up sales were to begin this evening, and if that wasn't enough reason to shop, Mother's Day would fall on Sunday. Mrs. Hanson was growing from one day to the next, and the rounder her belly became, the more was the adventure in finding clothes that fit and suited her.

She rose from her chair in the cubby and, kicking the pumps off her feet, she pulled Jed against her—"Hug?"—against the warm mass of her tummy, saying, "I was afraid you'd miss your bus this morning. What's all the fuss?"

"Two of my chickens are missing."

"You're sure?"

"There's only twenty-five left, I counted them."

Jed backed away from her then, mumbling hellos to the other women gathering around, overcome by his shyness even as he cast hungry glances at the candy bowls on their desks.

You never notice how many are pregnant until it's your turn, he thought. A sort of sorority springs up. Fran, Meg, three in the same office! All at the same time!

He lingered by the receptionist's desk, overhearing the baby chat, the updates on the morning sickness, on the theoretical underpinnings of breast feeding, on formula brands and the salutary properties of bananas and soda crackers.

Half an hour later, Willoughby having failed to meet them as planned, Jed and his mother descended in the elevator. If Willoughby could be relied on for anything these days it was to skip an engagement. Mrs. Hanson heaved a sigh of resignation, stepping forth into the lobby. "I suppose she won't be coming tonight, Jed."

In the Fred Meyer maternity department, a woman unknown to the Hansons, ample in her elbows and quick with a smile, having nothing better to do while her daughter sampled garments behind the slatted wooden door of one of the fitting rooms, watched Mrs. Hanson breeze back and forth in the severe pick to which her desperation had driven her: a deathly somber brown tunic. Mrs. Hanson raised and lowered her arms, doing a turn before the mirror, then she spun on her toes, gathered her waist in, and snuck a peek at her backside.

"Honey, you'll never get that big," the woman volunteered, in a tone of well-meaning frankness, and

Mrs. Hanson responded by dropping her pose and rolling her eyes in agreement.

"It's too big. Never mind that it's ugly and shapeless. Never mind that it's dull, sterile, baggy, insulting, and twenty per cent off. It's too big!"

On that note she stepped back laughing at her frumpy reflection in the mirror. Her new acquaintance joined in the laughter, and once they had understood each other, all was lost. Good taste knew no bounds. Jed's mother laughed so hard she lost her breath—she knocked hangers off the clothes rack, catching her balance. "This town," she cried. "It's this town!"

They dined at McDonald's and returned home without having found a single outfit that suited her. "Skunked," she complained, borrowing Jed's word for it—"skunked," though they had shopped at Fred's, Lamont's, Penney's, and two of the mall boutiques.

At this time of year in Fairbanks, in the middle of May, there are more than seventeen hours of daylight in the twenty-four, quite a lot of light, and so despite the lateness of the hour and the overcast in the sky—the weatherman had called for snow flurries—there could be no mistaking the details of the scene (a very curious scene) that met their eyes when they had ascended the driveway home.

Willoughby, Jed's sister, occupied the front porch in the most belligerent posture, brandishing Jed's air gun while lambasting a red squirrel that clung spread-eagled to the roof of the bird feeder plunging under the eaves.

"*Get off there! I won't tell you again!*"

The bird feeder pitched and spun so violently that the squirrel seemed to hold fast to it from fright or motion sickness more than from rodent intransigence or any desire it had to defy Willoughby. But her outrage made no allowances. Grandpa Henry, dodging the muzzle of the air gun, tried to soothe her indignation but to no effect. Willoughby shrieked at the squirrel and in the next moment Jed heard the familiar *pop* of the spring being released in his air pistol. She had fired a BB at point-blank range at the squirrel and missed.

"Willoughby!"

Mrs. Hanson ran up the sodden lawn in the sneakers she had changed into at work, with every step spattering her slacks with mud.

"What on earth—!"

"*Get off! Off!*"

Willoughby repeated her ultimatum and—*pop!*—didn't wait before letting fly another BB at the pesky squirrel. This time, hit in some furred quarter of its body, appalled and chittering crazily, the squirrel flung itself from the pitched, ginger-colored roof of the bird feeder, a cascade of sunflower seeds coming down around its head, and still smarting and jabbering, it raced past the Hansons, leaped onto the edge of one of the girthy logs that sided the house, and scampered across its length to safety.

"Serves you right," Willoughby shouted.

"Give me that gun."

Mrs. Hanson seized the BB pistol from her daughter who, unwilling to stand for any reproof beyond that implicit in her mother's voice, yanked open the front door and ran into the house, pulling it shut behind her.

Old Henry was left to defend his granddaughter. "She was only protecting the chickadees."

"I know it," Mrs. Hanson said, "but this isn't a toy. Jed, put this away."

The bird feeder still swinging at the end of its cable, Mrs. Hanson groaned stupendously. She rolled her neck, pressed the palm of her hand to her belly, then reached behind her with both fists and banged them into her lower back. "I want some chicken nuggets," she declared, "I'm starved."

Oh Christ but it dries you up, cracks your skin, blunts your heart, freezes your blood, wastes the spirit—the ice, the leafless wood, a golgotha!

Were there not many who had cried out in despair in the middle of winter in words such as these? But the spring this year had been fruitful of blessings, early and balmy as an Outside spring, with the thaw begun in late March soon followed by profusions of pussywillows, mosquitos and, already by May Day, a budding in the trees.

Grandpa Henry, arrived from California with his battery of medicines, monitored the onset of spring from their picture window, seeing in the advance and retreat of snow across the lawn the record of a battle.

"You couldn't see the ground there yesterday," he would say, extending his spotted, trembling forefinger, his old voice crackling from the depths of his afflicted larynx.

Spring! Jed raked up the autumn's leafy remnants. Dmitri the Siamese cat took to hunting voles outdoors. When the ice sheets slid off the roof of the house and shattered, Jed took care to throw the ice chunks downslope of their footpath, as his father had taught him to do, knowing the ice would melt by day and, refrozen at night, be treacherous in the morning.

He used a stickier ski wax in the spring. On the trails he had to pick up his skis over twigs and spruce cones and the droppings of dog teams. Before long, the moss itself cropped up through the snow. And the day came when Jed stepped out of his skis one last time and stood them against the side of the garage for the summer.

The shops roll up their rounds of parkas, the roadside ditches fill with runoff; drag races are held in the mud, the first Canada goose is spotted. Parents enroll their children in summer camp, you plug in the outside freezer in the nick of time, the tiny black springtails hop over your clothes, wasp nests hang ominously in the bare branches, wild bears stir, hunters oil their guns, greenhouses beckon, you flock to Creamer's Field and watch the long-legged cranes sinking through the air like crazy parachutists, the first ladybug you spot you just about jump and holler for joy for, May arrives, and you gaze up into the birch trees at the leaf buds revealed there, thousands of them, no, tens of thousands, no, skillions of them, green and moist and glittering in the sun.

Drivers on the Steese Expressway, glancing up from the road during the warm season, may notice eight yellow stars shining down on them from the west slope of Birch Hill, day and night, eight enormous stars of the finest grade concrete, cast in the earth in the shape of the Big Dipper and the North Star. In winter the memorial is buried in snow. But again in the spring the yellow stars come back upon the hill, the cemetery road is cleared of snow, and Jed and his mother visit the graveside of Mr. Hanson on Birch Hill. On a separate occasion Willoughby rides her bicycle to the cemetery and eats a bag lunch there.

The lawn-and-garden inserts in the newspaper, the men thronging the hardware stores—the spring brings many reminders of Jed's father. At his chores one day Jed discovers the brass case of a spent rifle cartridge, a relic of his father's target-shooting days, brought to light in the melting snow. He bends and examines the empty cylinder, he breathlessly turns the object in his palm as though assaying it for its gold content, and then he stows it in his pocket, marveling that his father once held it in his hand and no other human touch has intervened between that time and this.

One day in early April, while he was poking around outside in the casual way that a boy will when unconstrained by homework or chores, Jed came to the edge of the birch and spruce woods, beyond the garage, and as he was passing the old chicken coop built on skids there, an obscure but insistent tug on his attention, an unexpected prompting, brought him to a halt. Jed turned to the old chicken coop and stared. The feeling that had suddenly come over him, fetching him up in this way, was so mysterious that he wondered at its nature no less than at the sad spectacle of the chicken house itself.

What a sorry sight! In its heyday the coop had housed a hundred or more chickens. They had clucked, they had roosted here, they laid eggs, roistered, and scampered in the adjoining run. Jed remembered the feel in his hand of the first brown egg he had held—warm, full, slightly gritty to the touch. He recalled his father's laughter during the madcap minutes spent chasing the scattered flock across the lawn, Mr. Hanson's booming, high-spirited voice reaching him even now across the years. Over time Jed had all but forgotten the existence of the chicken coop, and he was shocked now by its deteriorated condition.

The fence of chicken wire that surrounded the coop bulged inward from the weight of the snow and fallen leaves piled against it. The coop door, overhung by an immense, shaggy spruce bough, was so warped and swollen that, even tugging with all his strength, Jed was barely able to wrench it open. His hair sprinkled with spruce needles, he peered in through the open door of the coop, blinking his eyes against the shade inside.

No sooner had he climbed over the sill and ventured into the coop than he planted his foot through a hole in the rotted floor. Yugh! The air in the coop was stale and musty, a stink of damp towels assailed his face, and as he shuffled in, hundreds of vole droppings—no, tens of thousands of the awful little pellets rattled in the newspapers under his feet. Jed poked to his left and his right, and he looked up into the corners of the ceiling, all the while holding his breath, or breathing as little as he could. The objects stored in the coop two winters ago after his father's death—the barbecue, the five-horsepower rototiller, the gardening tools, and the old toys the children had outgrown—it was all webbed together in a thick, choking, gritty web of—well, cobwebs!

Jed surrendered to a series of violent shivers, standing there in the damp dim coop. Its ruin ashamed him. The red bulb of the heat lamp dangled from its socket like an animal crawled from its burrow to die. The coop's neglect dispirited him, but he was aware, too, of a second impulse stirring in him, contrary to the first, or corollary to it, or certainly related to it in some way. And this answering motive kicked up in him as soon as he had returned outside, where the sight of a gray metal cylinder partly buried in the snow, recognizable to him as the top section of a chicken feeder— Jed stood it up and knocked the snow off it—provoked in him a bitter satisfaction and goaded him on to his grand idea.

Why not! The decay of the chicken house, was it really so relentless, so inevitable? Was there no point in trying to save it? It couldn't be more obvious to Jed what needed doing, and he set the project in motion that very day by telephoning the feed store in town and placing an order for thirty chicks.

For the rest of April, in all his spare time and with all his heart and energy, Jed Hanson busied himself with refurbishing the old chicken house. He ran outside after supper, he finished his homework early so that he could get on with the renovation. The objects that had been retired to the chicken coop after his father died—the barbecue, the rototiller, the outgrown toys—these Jed evicted from the coop, and he swept out the yellowed newspapers and the vole droppings, and he cleared those hideous cobwebs from the walls and ceiling.

A square of plywood, a hammer, and a handful of box nails were all he needed for patching the hole in the coop floor. He spent an entire Saturday afternoon disinfecting the interior of the chicken coop with a powerful detergent. The gangway in back of the chicken coop, a sloping wooden plank that communicated with the run outside, had rotted through and collapsed in the middle, and Jed mended this break with a plywood gusset. Next he restored the old roosting bars where his father had hung them in the coop corners. He oiled the metal fittings of the door and window; he screwed a new red ninety-watt bulb into the socket of the heat lamp; and he climbed on a stool outside and pruned back the great spruce bough that hampered the door's outward opening.

The telephone call came from the feed store in the middle of April. "Jed Hanson? Your chicks are in."

"Uhm?"

"That's a dollar a head for the Reds, eighty-five cents for the Cornish Cross."

Grandpa Henry, just arrived from California, accompanied Jed to the feed store, and for a lark, or because he was Jed's grandfather, he footed the bill for all thirty chicks.

They bought a month's ration of chick starter, too. At home they distributed the food in cardboard troughs cut from cereal boxes. Jed's family filed into the bathroom, now the nursery, and coddled the chicks, exclaiming how cuddly they were.

"Look how cute!"

"The little dickens!"

"Cute as a bug's ear!"

Even Willoughby thought so, at first.

Jed's optimism and hard work in restoring the chicken house were not lost on his family. Such devotion casts a spell of its own. His mother saw him out among the trees, dispersing armfuls of the leaves that he had raked away from the chicken-wire fence, and struck on the spot by an inspiration, she ran outside and asked him to drop the leaves by her old compost pile, if he would, she was planning to resume gardening this year.

Jed bent the fence back, plumb as he could. He drove metal posts into the ground at the fence perimeter. From the post tops he crossed heavy-gauge wires over the chicken run, and he tied strips of colored flagging to the wires, to spook the birds of prey. At last Jed gathered together all of the galvanized tops and bases of the chicken feeders and waterers that had been cast aside so carelessly in their season of neglect, and he hosed these off under a brisk jet of water and scrubbed them clean and propped them in the sunlight to dry.

Anyone would have forgiven Jed if at this point he had stepped back to admire his handiwork, but he had no sooner completed these tasks than it was time to remove the chickens from the family bathroom, which he had promised his mother he would do by the first of May.

The evacuation came none too soon as far as Willoughby was concerned. Thirty chicks, having neither indoor plumbing nor the ingenuity to use the human kind, no matter how diligently their keeper changes their litter of sawdust, will give off an odor peculiar to themselves, and many weeks later Willoughby could still be heard complaining of the ammoniac smell in the bathroom, venting her objections so loudly that her family knew exactly when she had gone to that special room to brush her teeth or to bathe by the exclamations of "Pyoo!" and "Yuk!" they heard coming from that quarter of the house.

The Hansons had always considered their picture window, a three-part bay window that looked on the front yard, to be by far the most important window in the house, because of the generous amount of light that it admitted in the winter when light is scarce. Unfortunately, the same window happened to be the backstop in line with the next squirrel that provoked Willoughby's wrath by laying siege to the bird feeder—which is to say that the window became the next victim of her ʙʙ pistol and her bad aim. The late Mr. Hanson had invested in a special quality of vacuum-sealed window whose side panel was effectively spoiled now: the tiny hole in the center of its outer pane, from which a pair of cracks radiated, was sure to admit moisture from the outside, and fogging and frosting of the window would follow as inevitably as winter follows fall. Jed was therefore surprised to learn from Willoughby that their mother had not scolded her for breaking the window, or in any way magnified her sense of wrong-doing by dwelling on the window's loss.

"I thought she'd blow up," Willoughby admitted.

In the chilly damp of late evening, Willoughby followed her brother from the house and, her hands buried in the side pockets of her Rocket Surplus army jacket, the kind then in style among her school friends, she accompanied him across the wet grass of the yard.

"In fact, as long as I don't shoot the house anymore, she says I can still use your ʙʙ gun, if you'll let me."

"She did?"

"Yuh-huh. Can I?"

"The ʙʙ gun?" His sister having, it seemed to Jed, so many private anguishes already, he wasn't eager to see any sufferings added to them, and though he wasn't innocent of the rivalries of a thirteen-year-old boy, he was happy the matter of the broken window had not cost her more grief than it had. "You can have it, if you want. I never use it. What are you going to do with it?"

"Chase the squirrels off. You're going to trap the fox, aren't you?"

"Who says I am?"

"Well, aren't you?"

But Jed having already entered the chicken run turned his attention to the startled flock before him. "Hah," he yelled, extending his foot and driving the birds toward the coop, "hey! Yah! Get in there!"

Willoughby joined him in the roundup, but she immediately repented of her helpfulness. "This is why you have to trap the fox," she yelled through a whirl-wind of feathers, "so we don't have to do this every night."

The young chickens gabbled and squawked, they pumped their bony little wings in panic, they puffed out their chests in bantam pride, all the while glow-ering at Jed and at Willoughby. With grudging obedi-ence they crowded toward the coop and entered it one by one, induced to hop up at the threshold or, if they preferred, to waddle up the gangway in the back. But the migration wasn't done before the few chickens that were still at large got it into their heads to bolt again.

"Look out!"

"Get that one!"

The rebellion spread. Pursued by Jed and Willoughby, the chickens scattered pellmell across the run, bumping into the fences, barreling into one another, miffed, maddened, screaming, spurring the ground and, what most disgusted Willoughby, splash-ing through their drinking water. Meanwhile the pul-lets and cockerels already in the chicken coop, hav-ing second thoughts about their confinement, filed to the open door of the coop and looked out. And seeing Jed's and Willoughby's backs turned, and catching the mood of exhilaration, they exploited the moment by hopping outside one after the other.

"Oh, God, this is crazy," Willoughby cried.

What with all the chasing, grabbing, screeching, stomping, smacking, stooping and sweeping that followed, Jed and Willoughby were full out of breath when they had finally hurled the last Cornish Cross into the chicken coop and slammed the door shut behind it.

Jed hastened around to the back of the coop and stood guard over the square hole from which the gangway descended.

"There is—no way," Willoughby panted beside him, "that we can do this every night."

Jed flicked his hand at the Rhode Island Red poking its beak forth. "Wait here, Will. And don't let anyone out."

He returned in a jiffy with a claw hammer, four nails, and a scrap of wood which he tacked up over the opening. "Sorry, chicks."

"Good night, pea-brains," Willoughby called.

A short while later, as they were returning the hammer to the tool box in the garage, Willoughby spotted, glowing in a corner of the garage, a hot-pink wheel, partly hidden in the hodgepodge of cast-off toys which Jed had moved here from the chicken coop as a first step in its renovation. She instantly became nostalgic.

"Look, Jed, my Beach Buggy. You think it still works?"

"That thing? I doubt it. I mean," seeing the charmed look on his sister's face, "you never know."

Before long they had freed the electric buggy from the surrounding junk and dragged it across the garage floor. Willoughby was giddy with excitement. "It was signaling to me, did you see, Jed? It wanted me to find it. Do you remember how it goes?"

"We'd have to charge the batteries."

"Will you?"

Jed was appalled. He looked at the silly decals that brightened the sides of the buggy, and the spruce pollen, birch seeds and dead mosquitos that clouded its toy windshield. The purple seat of molded plastic was just large enough to accommodate two six-year-olds sitting side by side, but no larger.

He popped open the hood of the buggy and glanced at the pair of six-volt batteries inside.

"We can check the fuses and stuff. The battery charger's probably in your closet. I guess we'll try it."

Clearly life was not going to be something you could make a single accommodation with and expect not to be troubled further by. Jed gazed up at the night shrouded in clouds. He knew this heavy coldness in the air. And while a snowfall in May was nothing extraordinary, not in Fairbanks, still, with certain exceptions—on the north side of the woodpile, or under the eaves where the snow had accumulated in heaps—with few exceptions the snow had all but vanished from the ground, and now, just when a welcome mildness was theirs at last, when the long and trying winter was left behind, it threatened to snow again.

No, he wouldn't be let off easily, not him or anybody else.

He returned alone to the chicken coop to switch on the heat lamp for his chickens. They didn't spook when he entered their precincts, but went about their business with an air of cozy confidence. They nestled down in their bedding or waddled about in that bandy-legged way they have, making guttural sounds of satisfaction while he positioned the heat lamp above them. Every bird seemed to have its place in this little domestic universe. They would appreciate the extra warmth tonight, and the lamplight would keep them from piling up on one another. Jed was pleased they were coming to trust him.

After he had said good night to his chickens, Jed, as he was walking past the garage, reached his hand out and, less by intention than reflex, rattled the animal traps that hung there, drawing his fingers across them as he passed. There were dozens of steel traps, Victor traps that had belonged to his father, badly rusted and dangling in bunches from pegs driven into the garage's stockade siding. On windy nights the old traps swayed and creaked and thud-thud-thudded against the unyielding log walls. They continued to swing and clatter when he had gone by, and for the rest of the evening he smelled the rust of their metal on his fingertips.

There was an occasion, seventeen months ago, when Jed took several of the traps down from the wall and amused himself by cocking them and triggering them with a stick. He had found a kind of sentimental fun in doing this, but was careless and left one of the traps out overnight, and he unintentionally caught a fox in it. The fox was released and likely survived, but even so, Jed had been slow to forgive himself for the accident, and whenever he saw a fox in the area he watched it for signs of a limp.

He had had nothing to do with the animal traps since then, but he hadn't forgotten the incident. Some events impress you the more for their peculiar timing, and this one, occurring a few months after his father's death, on Christmas Eve no less, was such an event. The fox, caught in these strange and memorable circumstances, had remained associated in Jed's mind with the free-ranging spirit of his father. Jed was not apt to believe in magic, but he had come to think of the animal traps—simple, deadly, cruel—as possessing a power he had paid a price for trifling with: if you failed to use caution in handling them, the wildness you hoped to lure and contain there could break loose in dangerous or unexpected ways.

Ah, but those were such dark days after his father died. There seemed to be a mad chaos at work in the heart of the world, and for months afterward his family suffered from bouts of dread and melancholy.

The pain lessened, with time. They were numbed to it, or simply got used to it. By and large things had not gone badly for the Hanson family. Jed and Willoughby had given up their home education and enrolled in the public schools. Mrs. Hanson had taken classes at the university and made a paralegal of herself. She dieted and lost weight, and in the fall she worked alongside Jed splitting firewood for their barrelstove. She had proved to be as brave and capable as her children could ask, and Jed no longer felt, as he once had, that he had lost his mother along with his father. Mrs. Hanson's most recent success was to sprout squash and tomato plants indoors; she had mapped out a plan of her entire garden in anticipation of June the first, which is sowing day in Fairbanks.

Now why, just when she had regained control of her life, she had gone and gotten pregnant, especially when beforehand it was so vitally important to her to shape up and lose weight, this was beyond Jed. Carrying a child made his mother busier with life than ever, though, and that couldn't be a bad thing. As for the prospect of having a baby brother or sister in the house, Jed was fairly neutral on the issue, he was so much older than the newcomer, it was hard to feel a tremendous enthusiasm or, on the other hand, to slouch around with the muted indignation of his sister Willoughby.

Willoughby had not exactly thrived since her father died. Their mother blamed Willoughby's misfortunes on the public schools and on the collision of her girlhood with her womanhood. Fifteen years old, Willoughby was pale, volatile, loving, blunt, defiant in her study of the trombone, and given to rhetorical questions the likes of—a particularly ferocious recent example:

"The guy who got her pregnant, you nitwit? It's that creep Mr. Allen. Who do you think it is?"

It was Willoughby who had devised the nickname Blind Boy for the one-eyed Cornish Cross whose eye his fellow chickens had pecked out. The nickname being memorable in its descriptiveness and pathos, it had stuck, and only in retrospect did Jed consider it likely that Willoughby had invented the name in a spirit of sarcasm.

Plump under the chin, not fat in the least but thinking herself overweight, Willoughby had taken it hard when she did not succeed as well as her mother on the diet they had embarked together on in the fall. Willoughby was plagued by a chronic pimple, too, in the little dell above her lip, where the mouthpiece of her trombone pressed, and Jed, knowing of her self-consciousness in regard to the blemish, was capable of alluding to it in moments of cruelty.

She kept her hair short, she wore gold and silver studs in her ears. All told, Jed was quite frightened of his sister. She could be so knowledgeable, so sure of herself. Take her theory about Mr. Allen. Jed was beginning to come around to it. But how had she known? She lashed out so unaccountably at times. And sometimes she made so little sense to him. This business of the Beach Buggy. Willoughby hadn't shown the slightest interest in that contraption for years. Mr. Hanson had dutifully charged the batteries at the prescribed intervals until he realized that Willoughby had outgrown the buggy and gone on to fitter amusements. And now, just when real automobiles were in reach, when in fact just months ago Willoughby was a passenger in a car whose driver, a high-school junior, was stopped and carted off by the Troopers for being intoxicated at the wheel, now on the eve of her own debutancy as a driver she drags out of mothballs her cockamamie, make-believe buggy that runs two miles an hour at high speed and in its heyday was the center-piece at a birthday party for six-year-olds!

Jed...Willoughby...their mother...They inhabited different worlds more than they used to. Mr. Hanson's death had brought them closer together in a way, but each had also received the chastening lesson of solitude: their pain must be borne separately, by each of them, alone. Nobody had been able to remove the hurt for Jed, not because they didn't want to, but because the pain seemed always to be there, a condition of things no human being could alter.

Jed tossed in his bed for many minutes that night, beset by his fears for his chickens. Had he done enough to protect them? No, he had certainly failed them. On the other hand, the coop was no flimsy hut, surely the birds were safe inside. Then again...

He was finally driven out of his bed altogether, and while the house slept, he tiptoed down the stairs and gazed out the window at the dim shape of the chicken house in the darkness, the reddish glow in its window... Poor Blind Boy, he thought. Poor chickens.

And again he felt in his stomach the sickening anguish he had felt that morning on discovering that two of his flock were missing. Poached! His shock, his anger and humiliation. Here one day, gone the next. *Two* chickens. A fine poultry-keeper Jed made. At this rate the pen would be empty and the flock reduced to no birds by June.

He had dedicated so much effort and hope to his flock, putting the mild despondencies of winter behind him, that now as he watched the first snow-flakes drifting down the sky it seemed as though winter were following winter and his faith being held up to ridicule.

2

In the morning a misguided redpoll bashed headlong into the picture window and—*bonk!*—it lay below in the new-fallen snow when Willoughby, who had heard the smack of its impact and rushed outside, knelt beside it to see what might be done. Cradled in her palm, the redpoll was alive, warm and open-eyed, but it wouldn't, or couldn't extend its wings and fly, and so with the idea of nursing it back to health she brought it into the house.

Jed joined his sister just as she was preparing egg yolks to feed to the wounded bird.

"Look how cute, Jed. You can feel it trembling. Come see."

Their mother was frying hash browns, eggs and sausages on the stove while Grandpa Henry sipped coffee and read the *News-Miner*. The house sizzled with the smells of a Saturday morning. Dmitri leaped up on the counter to see if there was any hope at all of his nailing the ailing songbird but was promptly knocked aside by—"Oh no you don't!"—an excitedly chattering Willoughby. She had lined a small box with a washcloth and laid the little finch inside. With her finger she stroked the red feathers of its cap.

"Will," Grandpa called to her, "there's another squirrel outside."

"Oh God, oh no, hold on," Willoughby cried.

She left the convalescent redpoll in Jed's care and went banging out the front door with her BB pistol in hand.

"You be careful of the windows," Mrs. Hanson shouted.

Pop! came the report of the air gun.

"Take that," Willoughby yelled.

Chitchitchitchitchit, the squirrel shot back.

"Did you get him?" Mrs. Hanson asked.

Willoughby returning to the kitchen, "Yep."

"Looks like Old Man Winter doesn't want to die," Grandpa remarked, observing the snowy lawn from the window.

"Like, nationally people commit suicide more around Christmas," Willoughby said, "but in Fairbanks they do it in the spring."

"All done but the hash browns," Mrs. Hanson announced. "You're off, Jed?"

He was pulling on his rubber boots at the door. "To check my chickens."

"Don't be long."

The squirrels darted under the porch boards when Jed emerged from the house, and thrust their heads up again as soon as he had crossed over and started down the path. Last night's snow was already melting, there was a pleasant patter of water dripping from the roof edges and the tree branches. His boots scooped through the wet snow to the grass, leaving a track of green ovals between the house and the door of the chicken coop.

"Good morning, good morning," he greeted the flock.

In numbering the birds, he lost count several times, and he pleaded with, entreated and begged them to be still. "Otherwise, I can't count you," he said. "I have to know if you're all here. Five, six, seven. They take a census in the Bible, did you know that? Ten, eleven. The whole United States has a census. Thirteen, fourteen—move it!—fifteen. Everybody has a census. Eighteen, nineteen..."

In the end all twenty-five of his surviving chickens were safe and accounted for. But, as he discovered when he returned outside, not everything was well. What at first glance had appeared to be a random disturbance in the snow around the chicken coop—Jed crouched to have a closer look—was actually an involved set of fox tracks. Although the snow was quickly melting, and although his own footprints had eclipsed some of the fox tracks, the remaining record couldn't be misinterpreted. The fox had sniffed at the door and walls of the chicken coop; had crawled between the skids underneath it; had even had the gall to dig snow and dirt away from the side of the coop at a point adjacent to the rotten spot on the floor within. A busy fox!

This was the surest evidence to date that a fox, not any of the other suspects, certainly not a bogeyman, had been preying on Jed's chickens. Jed's suspicions fell into place now and his doubts withdrew, but as he strode back to the house, he felt oddly reluctant, almost helpless in the face of his resolve. What he regretted was the timing of his discovery. In the Fairbanks game management unit, the season for trapping red fox had expired with the month of February, which effectively put Jed, through no desire of his own, at loggerheads with the law.

"While you're dressed, Jed, would you take this out?" His mother met him at the door and, speaking to him in a confidential whisper, handed him the cardboard box in which Willoughby's redpoll lay dead.

"Oh, no."

"Yes, I'm afraid so."

Breakfast was a solemn affair. The forks and knives kept up a shameless conversation, but few words were spoken, out of respect for the deceased redpoll and for Willoughby, who had become the bird's devoted nurse and its mourner in the space of an hour. Jed had buried the creature in a niche formed by the buttress roots of a giant spruce tree, and he'd noted the tree's location so that he might point it out to Willoughby one day.

Grandpa Henry made two trips to the bathroom during breakfast—about average, for him. As he had neglected to don his battery pack, the slim amplifiers of his hearing aids were useless, and in consequence everything had to be shouted to him.

"Dad, can I get you more coffee?"

Willoughby, who was subject to fits of ferocity even on the mildest days, despised the squirrels more than ever for their marauding ways, and twice interrupted her breakfast to drive them off the porch, pelting them with BBs fired from the air pistol her brother had given her. Jed was scheduled to attend an afternoon fundraiser, a Spring Car Wash some students from his school were holding in the Sam's Club parking lot, and he invited Willoughby to come along.

"No, thanks. You think my car's ready?"

"Your car?"

"My Beach Buggy."

"Oh." *That* racy thing.

Jed rose from the breakfast table and knelt by the electrical outlet where he had left the pair of batteries charging overnight. The AC adaptor was warm to his touch. He disconnected the batteries and carried them outside to the garage where he and Willoughby installed them under the buggy's purple hood.

By the time Jed had returned to the house, Grandpa Henry had put his own battery pack in order. It bulged squarely under the breast of his pullover sweater. Twin wires looped up to his ears.

"Looks like I'll have to get some traps out," Jed announced, sitting and speaking his mind.

"Not another chicken gone," his mother said.

"Fox tracks everywhere."

"Do you have to, Jed?"

"He has to protect his chickens," Grandpa said.

"Fish and Game," his mother said, "don't they handle these things?"

Jed shook his head, muddled and uncertain. It would be nice if somebody else would take care of his problem. He poured himself a glass of milk and drank it, thinking of his father. To be resolute wasn't always automatic with Jed—perhaps it isn't with most people. To be resolute must be a conscious thing.

"I guess I'll be able to handle it," he said.

Well then you'd better be surer of yourself than you were at the beginning of this affair, he thought. Three or four days had passed before he even realized the first chicken was missing. A single bird in an energetic flock of thirty, dispersed across the area of the chicken run, doesn't make a big impression by its presence or absence. When he finally noticed that a chicken was gone, he immediately blamed the foul play on Dmitri. He cornered the mischievous cat, grabbed him by his carnivorous throat, peered into his eyes and... was regarded warmly in return. If Dmitri showed the whites of his teeth, that was only because of the stranglehold Jed held him in.

A second chicken vanished. Dmitri, on the night it happened, had as solid an alibi as any suspect could hope for, Jed himself having locked Dmitri in the bathroom that night.

So Jed blamed the owls and hawks. It distressed him to do so. The idea of birds preying on their fellow birds, especially on the lowly and misunderstood domestic fowl, whose identity as a bird is probably treated as a joke in the higher avian circles—the idea of a bird-eat-bird world was distasteful to Jed, but he took the precaution of suspending additional wires over the chicken run, and he doubled in number the strips of pink and blue flagging that hung from the wires, in order to startle, deceive and repel even the rashest, hungriest raptor.

A third chicken disappeared. Jed called around to the neighbors. By chance had anyone's dog been loose on the night in question?

Foxes were suspect of course. Foxes are always suspect. There was the red fox Jed and Willoughby and Grandpa Henry had seen trotting by the coop one day at the beginning of May. But no definite evidence pointed to the culprit, and even after the recent raid, when Blind Boy and a fifth chicken went missing, the fate of the pair remained a mystery. The fox tracks in the snow this morning offered a compelling case, but even this evidence could be called circumstantial, and Jed was frankly perplexed.

"How did he slip through the fence? I can't figure it out. Did he climb over? The tracks don't tell."

"You bet," Grandpa said. "That's why they're called sly foxes."

"For heaven's sake," Mrs. Hanson gasped, "look at this."

Jed's mother had stopped clearing the table and was staring out the picture window. Jed and Grandpa Henry joined her there and were treated to the sight of Willoughby zipping around the lawn in her old Beach Buggy.

"Hmm, she doesn't really fit," Grandpa remarked.

No, she didn't. She sat crowded into the well of the car, out of all proportion to it, hunkering over the steering wheel, her knees protruding up at the sides, driving in a broad circle on a part of the lawn from which the snow had already melted. When Willoughby came around the circle, madly turning the little steering wheel, her family saw the delight that animated her features. They watched her with grave attention, as though they were listening for something, or as if they had heard, or fancied that they heard, a small, childish voice crying out *Mom! Dad! Look at me! Look at me!*

Jed would have given two, or even three of his chickens—sacrificed them—hurled them into the gorge at Hurricane Gulch—impaled them on a pole and let the eagles ravage them—anything, for a handshake with fate—anything, if he could have prevented what happened next.

It began when one of the stout plastic wheels of the buggy caught on the downhill side of a ridge of wet, tangled grass. The buggy lost traction and became stuck in the middle of a turn. Willoughby tried to back the car up—it had a reverse gear, it was no inexpensive toy—but the layer of snow behind her threatened to mire her even further and there just wasn't the room she needed to gather the momentum for an escape. So naturally, after spinning the wheels again, Willoughby, in her Rocket Surplus army jacket, uncramped herself from the seat of the buggy and climbed out. She picked up the nose of the car, swung it free of the grassy obstruction, gave the buggy a shove to put it on course, and dropped every one of her hundred thirty pounds into the seat of the buggy and broke its chassis the instant she did so.

The buggy collapsed. The right front wheel popped off its axle, wobbled free, and rolled over on its side, leaving the car sitting cock-eyed in the grass with Willoughby inside it.

"Oh, dear," Mrs. Hanson said.

Willoughby's first visible response to this catastrophe was to look toward the house where her mother, brother and grandfather happened to be standing at the window. They would certainly have ducked if they had had the time or the foresight to do so.

"Oh, no," Mrs. Hanson said.

"Is she crying?" Grandpa said.

Her buggy abandoned in the grass, Willoughby came limping toward the house, the cuffs of her too-long sleeves clutched in her fingers. For no obvious reason, however, she then about-faced and went wandering down the driveway in the opposite direction.

"That does it," Mrs. Hanson said.

"Does what?" Jed said.

"I'm going to Anchorage. I'm taking Willoughby with me."

"Anchorage?"

His mother turned from the window. "I have some shopping to do."

"We went shopping yesterday."

"There's been no shopping in this town since Nordstrom closed."

"What about the new Sears?" Jed followed her to the bottom of the stairs. "K-Mart has maternity clothes."

"Shops and shopping aren't the same thing. Willoughby needs a weekend off. So do I."

At the top of the stairs Mrs. Hanson ducked into her bedroom, and before long she descended carrying an overnight bag stuffed with the essentials of travel. Grandpa Henry had remained at his post by the window keeping an eye on Willoughby outside.

"She's walking down by the road, Liz."

"That's all right, I'll pick her up."

She kissed her son and father, stepped into her shoes at the door, flipped her purse under her arm, and shouldered her bag by the strap. "You men take care of yourselves. Grandpa will drive you to the Car Wash, Jed. We're off to the airport. Call the Holiday Inn in Anchorage and book us a room, will you? Goodbye! See you tomorrow night. Goodbye!"

Outside, as soon as his mother had driven off after Willoughby, before the slush had even settled in the driveway, Jed turned to the side of the garage where the animal traps hung and lowered three of them, three single-long-spring fox traps, from their pegs. These he brought into the house and boiled in the oversize enameled caldron which his family traditionally used for canning their jams and jellies. The chains, the springs, the steel jaws of the traps banged around in the caldron as they cooked, and the water took on the reddish color of their rust.

Jed tonged the boiled traps from the caldron, and, in order to keep the man-scent off them, he wouldn't let Grandpa Henry handle the traps, and he himself wore cotton gloves on his hands as he carried the traps outside and hung them to breathe in the open air.

Next he visited the chicken coop and examined the site from different angles, reflecting on a strategy for his trap set. He had to be in town soon, to lend his hand at the fundraiser, but before leaving he fed and watered his flock and made certain they were safely fenced within the run. Lastly he rummaged in the chest freezer in the garage and found a Ziploc bag containing the flecked and feathered wing of a ruffed grouse. Shaking the ice crystals loose in the bag, Jed hurried back to the house and left the frozen wing on the kitchen counter to thaw.

Grandpa Henry made quite an impression on Jed's friends in the Sam's Club parking lot that afternoon. In his pullover sweater and space-age hearing aids, with a bump at his sternum where his battery pack protruded, Grandpa was not the least bit awkward with Jed's friends, and he even took his turn waving the CAR WASH sign at the College Road traffic and manning the nozzle of the water hose while Jed and his gang went among the parked cars and trucks with their buckets of soapy water and their wet rags and sponges.

Grandpa Henry was a large man whose strong natural constitution, solid limbs and keen eyesight had brought him honor in his active years as an athlete and soldier, an aeronautical draftsman, a husband and father. Truly, however, Grandpa didn't look well today, not well at all. For one thing, he had lost a great deal of weight in the course of his illness, and he wore suspenders to keep his trousers up and his shirt from trailing under his sweater. His complexion was chalky at one moment and weirdly blue the next; he often seemed dazed, his responses were slow; the pains of arthritis wracked his knee and his ankle; and sometimes when he spoke his voice emerged so small and scratchy from his throat that Jed, when he heard it, involuntarily winced.

The cancer that plagued Grandpa Henry required him to swallow a daily deluge of medicines and to make frequent visits to the men's room. Fortunately the doorwoman at Sam's Club saw them washing cars out there in the parking lot and didn't challenge Henry for a membership card each time he approached to use the facilities inside. Grandpa's stated purpose in coming from California to Alaska was to be with his family during his recuperation and to help around the house in whatever ways he could during the term of his daughter's pregnancy. He had settled comfortably downstairs in the fold-away bed and after three weeks there was no indication that he would leave any time soon. Since he was Jed's only living grandparent, and especially now that they were together for the whole of Saturday, just the two of them, Jed found himself wanting to watch over the old man, and one of his ambitions was to plan and cook the night's meal. On their way home from the Car Wash they stopped at the market so that Jed could run inside and buy some fresh ginger.

"You have to have the ginger," he explained at home, peeling the root under his grandfather's observant eye, "it's the secret ingredient. You want to cut carrots for us? It's really easy, I'll show you. Ruffed grouse is so tender, you don't have to marinade it, but we can pour some wine over the breast if you want. Can you reach the bottle? Good. Wine is good for old people, that's what I heard. You want pepper? Great..."

Willoughby and Mrs. Hanson weren't home to interrupt or be bossy with them at the table, and Jed and Grandpa Henry were more talkative than usual that night. They dined on a stir fry of pearly white ruffed grouse with onions, ginger and julienne carrots served over a mound of white rice. Their mealtime conversation touched on Jed's studies at school, the merits of the biathlon as a sporting event, a powerful new hearing aid on the market, Willoughby's fixation with the squirrels, and Grandpa Henry's single-handed capture of more than two dozen German soldiers during the war in which he had fought fifty years ago.

"Well, it wasn't quite that way," old Henry laughed. He laid his fork down on his plate and moved his broad hands to illustrate the position of the troops.

"The Germans were already trapped in this forest. Our reconnoitering units had flanked them on either side. There was a German fellow waving a white flag at us from the trees. I was the radio man, so Company Headquarters sent me into the clearing with my radio. No one knew what was going to happen. Pretty soon a

German soldier comes out of the forest and gives me his pistol. The next thing you know, they're all coming out from behind the trees and giving me their weapons."

"So what did you do?"

"What I did?"

"Yeah."

"Well, I got on the radio and called for some chewing gum."

"Chewing gum?"

"You betcha. A peace offering."

"Oh."

Grandpa nodded. "You betcha," he said. He considered the pills in the palm of his hand, then he popped them into the back of his throat and chased them down with a swallow of ginger ale.

"Say," he said afterwards, "there's that old bird wing on the counter where you left it. You going trapping tonight?"

Jed hesitated, looking out the picture window. He still had several hours of light to work by.

"Having second thoughts?" Grandpa said.

"It's illegal to trap a fox this time of year," Jed said. "It's too late for it. Or too early. Same thing. The fur's not thick. The fox might have a family. The boy and the girl fox, they both take care of the children, I'd hate breaking the family up and..."

Jed stopped himself, realizing what a torrent of words had poured from his mouth. It was as though he had expected Grandpa Henry to release him from an obligation that Grandpa Henry had never imposed on him.

"Well," Grandpa said, "if I understand you, Jed, those rules were written with trappers in mind. But, like you said, you're not trapping the critter for a fur-bearer, you're trapping him for preying on your chickens. Isn't that so?"

"Yes."

"You don't feel right about it."

As a matter of fact, Jed had pushed the affair of the fox and chickens entirely from his mind while they were in town and he regretted having to face it squarely again at home. But squarely he must. There was the memory of Blind Boy and the other slain chickens to consider; there was Jed's duty to the surviving flock and to his own aspirations as a poultry-keeper. These were his thoughts as he remustered his resolve and rose from the table.

Just beyond the chicken coop, at the edge of the woods that surrounded the Hanson clearing, there grew a large and hoary birch tree whose speckled trunk, host to many strange funguses, leaned toward the woods at such an overbearing angle that over time the earth itself had heaved up around the rim of its roots, causing a hollow to form on the near side of the tree at its base. It was here that Jed knelt with a garden trowel and began to dig.

He scooped aside bunches of old wet leaves and with gloved hands troweled into the earth at an angle until he had opened a hole to the depth of the trowel blade, a narrow hole such as one a wild animal might dig as a cache for its carrion. The grouse wing, which he had smeared with dinner drippings before leaving the kitchen, he buried at the bottom of this freshly dug hole, and a few inches from the entrance he scraped out a level depression in which he positioned the trap itself.

From the swivel at the end of the trap, Jed routed a drag wire to the nearest cornerpost of the chicken pen. He bedded the trap firmly in the depression, then cocked it by forcing its spring down and, with the jaws open, setting the trigger ever so lightly to the edge of the circular pan.

There.

Jed sprinkled dirt over the fox trap and tossed some leaves over it. Then he backed up, studied the approach to the trap, and poked a few long twigs into the ground around the hollow at the base of the tree. These were to help guide the fox toward the trap but without arousing its suspicions.

There, that should do it.

He turned to the trio of Rhode Island Reds who were sternly eyeing him from the enclosure of the chicken run. "Don't you think so?" he said.

These three had been no less absorbed in watching Jed through the spaces in the chicken wire than he in setting the trap, but their truce ended with Jed's announcement of the evening curfew:

"In the coop! Get in the coop!"

The run exploded in a riot of protest. The chickens hated the roundup with as much passion as a free people hates martial law.

"Coop, coop, coop!"

Twenty-five hysterically bawling chickens hurry-scurried around Jed with all the color and decorum of a flock of birds gone cuckoo. They had a way of flinging themselves out of his reach just when he stooped to grab them. And for the next half hour, without the blessing of Willoughby's help this time, Jed chased those chickens across every inch of fenced ground and was tripped, trampled, battered, pecked, scratched and befouled before at last he had corralled them in the coop and could lean his hand on its lapped wood siding and catch his breath.

"Now what do you suppose," Grandpa Henry posed the question to him that evening, "Saint Francis would have done about mosquitos?"

"Hmm..."

"Sure. A man like that, going around without a shirt on in mosquito country, getting bit all the time, what'll he do?"

Jed spooned some Rocky Road ice cream into his mouth, hearing the whine, now near, now farther overhead, of a mosquito that, loose in the house, had for the last several minutes been persecuting him and Grandpa at the table.

"Slap them?"

"Long as he's human he will. He wasn't a saint until he died, if I remember correctly."

"Maybe he'd talk to them first."

"Oh, sure, he'd talk to them. They've loads of four-letter words in Italian."

The mosquito dive-bombed Jed's ear again and Jed swung his spoon at it and missed. When they were done, he carried their dessert plates to the kitchen sink.

"Every time you go by that window, you're looking for your trap," Grandpa remarked.

"It's bugging me."

"Want to know something?"

"What?"

"You're not too young to hear this, but I guess you probably know it already."

"What is it?"

"Well, lots of times," Grandpa said, "things aren't as simple as we want them to be. Like black and white, and yes and no. Rules and laws are a good thing, and without laws we'd be sunk. But there are lots of laws, Jed. That's what you have to keep in mind. It confuses the heck out of me, and I'm a lot older than you. There's a law like a trapping law which is written in the books. And there's a law like the one that says a young man protects his flock of chickens, which isn't. There's God's laws, too. There's laws we don't understand, there's laws we think are stupid, there's laws that look crazy, there's even laws that break other laws."

"It sounds confusing," Jed admitted.

Grandpa Henry laughed. "Well, I'll be turning in soon, I'm pretty tired. But there was a story I wanted to tell you. All this with the fox and chickens reminds me of it. Got a minute?"

"Sure."

"It happened in the war," Grandpa said. "We were marching through the countryside, and we came to some farmhouses the Germans had abandoned. The fight had taken a good turn for our side, and the Germans were running away from us. Well, there were lots of farmhouses in the country, and there were lots of eggs in the farmhouses. And we took the eggs, we ate them. Yep, as many eggs as we could, we stole them and ate them. Boiled them, kept them in our K-ration boxes so they wouldn't get crushed.

"There were some boys who took more than eggs, too, let me tell you. It was wrong. Very wrong. That's why they say war is hell, Jed, all the laws get turned around. We'd seen our boys' bodies piled by the bridge where we crossed the river. Those were the same villages and farmhouses the Germans were shooting mortars at us from."

Grandpa Henry fell silent and got the faraway look in his eyes that Mrs. Hanson blamed on all the medications he took. Jed encouraged him to continue. "Bombs?"

"Yes, a kind of bomb, Jed. Mortar shell comes in, it whistles a little, you dive for cover."

And with those words Grandpa Henry pushed himself up from the table. He stood a minute, swaying and letting his body stabilize. Then, as he always did before he went to bed, he pulled the hearing aids out of his ears, saying, "Well, I guess I've heard enough for one day."

That was the night the fox came to the old birch tree on the Hanson place. He swept through the forested acres and crept close along the shadowed verge. He prowled the woods in the blue dusk of midnight, threaded his way through the alder thickets, and padded across the mossy glades.

Jed had been reading a biography for most of the last two hours and his eyes itched from the concentration of it. When he saw the fox, he turned his book over on the table and took up his binoculars. The fox had smelled the bait and didn't dally before approaching the grand old birch tree that branched over the outskirts of the chicken run. The fox circled close from the far side of the tree and raised his forelegs on the earthen bank at its base.

He dipped his nose over the hollow on the near side of the tree and traced in the air the smell of the hidden grouse wing. He was cautious; didn't step down in the hollow, but glanced to his left at the chicken run, just pounces away from him, then raised his eyes and gazed at the log house where young Jed Hanson sat watching from the picture window.

And still the fox didn't step down in the hollow. Nosing the air, he wouldn't get off that safe mound of earth and decay where the roots splayed down from the old birch tree.

The fox lowered his nose across the trunk of the birch and smelled of the air in the hollow again. But something was wrong with the smell in the hollow: something had turned in that air. There was a familiar odor, of game, of bird, of meat, of meat on the verge of putrefaction, but it mingled with a trace odor that fouled it and cast a man-sized shadow on the night.

The fox glanced again at the chicken coop. He gazed at the log house that dominated the clearing. He put forth his muzzle from the far side of the tree and tested the air in the hollow. And he stayed for such a long time in this way that Jed eventually reasoned that the trap had been sprung and the fox had been caught.

The fox lingered, not indifferent, but looking at nothing in particular, perhaps listening for the mews of its kits in the distant den. At last Jed believed that the fox had truly been caught, and he fetched his .22 rifle and hurried outside.

But the fox had lost interest. And even as Jed trotted toward him across the yard, the animal trotted away in the gray-toned night.

Indeterminate sounds, whisperings and clickings, emerged from the night woods. A flap of birch bark scraped against a branch. A spruce cone completed a fall to earth it had begun months earlier. Jed, standing over the undisturbed bait hole, turned his head with every new sound, thrilling with rapid, instinctive shivers. Staring among the trees, he heard the rustle of the fox a second time, and this time he followed it in, in past the edge of the woods. Soon he glimpsed the muted auburn of the fox's fur, a sleek horizontal flitting among the trees, among the dark spruce and the paler birch.

When he lost sight of the fox, Jed crouched in the moss and waited. Wide-eyed, he pressed his hand to the earth and strained to penetrate the gloom. The chickens squawked nearby; the neighbor's hounds were barking in the distance. The dogs had only just ceased their spatting and the quiet returned to the woods when the leaves near Jed exploded in a violent thrashing.

The upheaval lasted for upwards of thirty seconds. Jed didn't breathe in that time. The shadows spun, they crackled, the shrubs whipped around in the surrounding darkness, Jed staring blindly into it, unable to locate the source of the ruckus, his leg muscles convulsing in spasms. Knowing the fox was close, he released the safety on his rifle, and had hardly done so before a terrific shriek went up in the woods, a high-pitched cry of pain that raised the blood on his back.

What a havoc! Jed reached for the tree trunk nearest him. The screaming didn't stop. It echoed among the trees, it rose over their tops, he fell forward listening to it, peering sideways under the branches, pressing himself to the earth in a futile effort to escape it. The screaming loudened, climbing in pitch and purity, then shrilling to a crescendo before it abruptly ceased.

The ensuing silence was almost as horrifying.

"Oh, my God," Jed whispered.

He turned to the house, he turned at a run. He hadn't gone two steps before he saw the fox. He stopped. He raised his rifle.

It was one o'clock in the morning, too dim out for shooting with confidence at a target sliding among the trunks of so many trees. But Jed clearly saw through his rifle scope, if only for a moment, the limp form of a snowshoe hare dangling from the fox's jaws. The hare's rear legs hung to one side, the long-eared head lolled on the other. The fox had found a meal. And he trotted home with it, his gait easy, his head drawn up, and the red mane of his fur fluffing out in the night breeze.

3

Sunday was Mother's Day and they couldn't decide on a gift for Mrs. Hanson. The problem was one of an abundance of choices. Jed and Grandpa Henry toured every greenhouse in Fairbanks and late in the afternoon came home with a potted rosebush, ten bags of chicken manure, and a hanging planter overflowing with blue forget-me-nots.

"She loves chicken manure," Jed assured Grandpa Henry. "She'll build her zucchini hills from it. It makes the flowers pretty. Don't worry."

Jed also bought a urine-based fox lure in the trapping supplies section of the hardware store. That evening after checking on the well-being of his chickens, he sprinkled the fox urine around the bait hole of his trap. The new smell would permeate the trap and mask whatever man-scent had betrayed him on the night before.

He had gone to bed so late last night, with the image of the killed hare so fresh in his mind, that his sleep had been fitful and all too brief, and consequently he had dragged his feet all day, all the more sluggishly because Grandpa Henry had awakened him early in the morning to attend the service at Zion's Hope, where he might have indulged in a harmless and spiritually soothing nap except that he felt badgered by the pastor's homily on the meaning of Mother's Day and the special value of parenthood and marriage.

"*We're* a fatherless household," Jed muttered afterwards as they drove out of the church parking lot. His enjoyment of Kool-Aid and donuts in the downstairs social room had ascended no higher than his stomach. He wondered how many of the congregation discussed Hanson family business at their supper tables.

"Your father dying is very different from what the pastor's talking about," Grandpa said.

"Mom's going to have a baby," Jed replied, "and she isn't married."

There was a touch of defiance in Jed's voice when he spoke. Grandpa Henry had no easy answer for the observation and drove on in silence.

"Did she tell you," Jed asked him, "if it's the lawyer at her office?"

"Come again?"

"Mr. Allen."

"Oh, Mr. Allen." The battery pack suddenly needed repositioning on Grandpa's chest. Grandpa twisted the earphones in his ears and lightly rapped himself on the side of the head, to clear his hearing, or something. "She didn't entrust that information to me, Jed."

"Willoughby thinks it's him."

"And you?"

"I'm starting to. Know what happened Friday?"

Jed had met Mr. Allen at a half dozen office parties and had come to recognize him for his unpredictable standoffishness, his fondness for wry jokes, and his preference for diagonally striped neckties which off-set the softnesses of his face, his fleshy cheeks and dark eyes with their melancholy downturn. A partner at the law firm, Mr. Allen was of medium build, quite elegantly handsome, with most of his hair intact and most of it still black.

Jed liked him. The lawyers were generally an indifferent bunch, scornful of the staff children, but Mr. Allen had contrived to take an interest in Jed and Willoughby, or he gave this impression by asking questions of them or sharing whatever amusing observation was at hand. Mr. Allen was said to be a bachelor, and Mrs. Hanson had spoken highly of him at the supper table, though not, come to think of it, recently.

On Friday, when Jed rendezvoused with his mother at the law offices, Mr. Allen had brushed by him in the corridor near the receptionist's desk—presumably on his way to pull a file or to drop a letter in the mail basket, or whatever. Mrs. Hanson and Fran and Meg happened just then to be tattling on about their pregnancies, and two things happened. One, Mr. Allen leaned down in passing and whispered to Jed, "I think it's something in the water." And two, as Mr. Allen slid past, Mrs. Hanson's carriage visibly stiffened: she pulled in her backside and raised high her chin but didn't otherwise acknowledge him.

These small evidences, taken together and in retrospect, may have meant more than they appeared, and since Friday Jed was apt to credit a little more his sister's theory—a dogma, with her—that Mr. Allen was the culprit, the silent partner in their mother's pregnancy.

"Well," Grandpa listened patiently to Jed's analysis, "maybe so. It's easy to offer advice, if Liz asks me for it, but this isn't something your grandpa's going to butt into, not if he knows what's good for him."

"But shouldn't she tell us? I don't know why she doesn't tell us."

"I don't know either, Jed. There was a time when the world had scoundrels and gentlemen in it, and everybody knew which was which. Everybody knew what was expected of them in those days. It's not so easy anymore. People are mean and lonely and full of pain. The pastor's only doing his job."

Jed had a recurrent daydream in which, by dint of writing many letters, of making telephone calls and online searches, he and Willoughby finally persuade their mother's unknown suitor to reveal himself and assume his rightful place in their household. Their sleuthing pays off, and in the end the mysterious lover always turns out to be—Jed's father, Mr. Hanson.

"She should just tell us," Jed said, slumped in his seat and scowling out the window.

This was the second night on which the red fox visited the old birch tree on the Hanson place.

It was five minutes past eleven, by the clock on the microwave oven, and Jed was more than midway through his biography of the scientist-explorer Roy Chapman Andrews. He had read a good chunk of the book tonight because Grandpa Henry had retired early to his bedroom after bruising himself in a fall. They had been carrying the rosebush and forget-me-nots into the house for the night for safekeeping—there is still the chance of a killing frost in May—when Grandpa Henry, crossing the threshold with the fiber pot in his arms, the fragrant rose and its attendant lavender buds playing under his nostrils, became dizzy in the doorway and fainted.

The old man looked very discombobulated, sitting on the floor with his strength so suddenly given out, his hearing aids jarred loose in his ears. Jed was torn between helping him to his feet and pretending not to have seen him fall. The incident dampened Willoughby's and Mrs. Hanson's homecoming, for obvious reasons. When mother and daughter entered the house by the front door, lively and full of laughter— "We're home!"—back from their travels and ready to show off the clothes they had bought in Anchorage, Jed was forced to tell them about Grandpa Henry's accident, and they took to whispering and tiptoeing around the house after that. Even so, the Mother's Day rose was only slightly bent (the bush had tumbled to the floor along with Grandpa), the soil was back in its pot, and the rose was still as sweet-smelling as a rose can be.

And so the house slept, and Jed was left alone with the fox. With the fox and with his own quickening heartbeat. He saw the animal clearly in his binoculars. A big fox, between color phases. There were patches of black fur in the rear of the animal, and the outside tips of his ears were black too. His belly and shoulders were orange.

The fox angled directly toward the old birch tree where the trap was set and a hint of carrion perfumed the air. He was bolder than last night, pushing forward from the far side of the tree, stretching his paw down toward the bait hole. Mmmm, he smelled those tasty shreds of meat adhering to the shoulder of the grouse wing; the bait had ripened nicely and the fox scooted around smelling it—that, and the fresh fox lure which Jed had sprinkled on the ground six hours earlier.

Jed leaned forward resting his elbows on the table to steady his binoculars. *Come on, step on it, step on the pan.*

The chickens must have sensed the fox out there and raised a squawk about it. The fox, alarmed, pricked up his ears, standing high on the hump of earth at the foot of the birch tree. He pressed his lean nose through the air, tracing a circle with it, and retracing the circle, and then having gotten whatever reassurance a fox needs, he returned to the challenge of filching the hidden grouse wing.

And filch it he did.

It happened swiftly, gracefully, Jed never quite saw how. He saw exactly what his eyes took in, and what his eyes took in produced a mortifying wonder in him. The fox reached his paw down into the hollow at the base of the birch tree and deftly dug with it, and when he lit on the other side of the hollow, all in one motion, in the moment before he leaped away through the woods, the shape of the grouse wing was visible clamped in his jaws.

Jed refused to believe it. The angle of the bait hole in the ground should have made it impossible for the fox to retrieve the buried grouse wing except by approaching from the front. Impossible.

He ran outside, dropped to his knees, and thrust his hand in the bait hole thinking the grouse wing would be there. Nope. No grouse wing. The trap was unsprung. Jed verified this by sweeping the dirt and leaves off it and stabbing the stub of a branch on the center of the pan. *Clap!* The jaws snapped shut on the stick.

The fox had bypassed the trap and lifted the grouse wing from the hole as easily as a wind does a leaf. Jed knelt in the encroaching darkness, measuring his own clumsiness against the fox's light-footedness, and, stung by the comparison, he flung the trap aside, the stick still caught in its jaws.

The skewed old birch tree that loomed above him, its uppermost branches lost in the darkness, was a tree that Jed had never known not to be there. It had held him in its lap when he was too young to climb it, and its stubbled bark had scuffed his smooth cheek—how many times? To Jed the old birch tree, being commensurate with his existence, seemed to grow out of the deepest roots of his memory, or he from its, so that, in a strange way, his kneeling at its foot was already an act of recollection, familiar to him and intimate, to be recalled as he saw it now, his shoulders shaking lightly from the breath of the night going through him, gazing up into the height of its branches and conscious of the link it forged between him and the masterly fox, its spring leaves rustling in untold numbers in the night air.

The squirrels had been having a field day, what with Willoughby's weekend absence from the house, and early on Monday morning Willoughby decided enough was enough, and in the name of the songbirds whose protectress she had become she marched out on the porch to restore order.

These squirrels were the brashest animals. They pilfered the sunflower seeds from the bird feeder but were never satisfied until they had wallowed in the mound of black hulls fallen to the ground below. Emboldened by the spring, they had annexed this territory for themselves, at the same time occupying the porch, the porch roof, and the choice buffer zone of earth in front of the picture window, an area dotted with hiding places, spy holes and escape routes.

There was no use sneaking up on these squirrels because they always alerted one another to your presence. If you tapped on the window to annoy them, they jerked around and glared at you with brown furious bulging eyes. They whistled at Dmitri, ridiculing his attempts to stalk them; they reinsulated the house on their own terms, dragging tatters of yellow fiberglass into the spruce trees; and as for respecting human boundaries, a squirrel's proudest moment was in bounding across the porch roof to a point directly over the bird feeder and sliding down the cable it hung from—yippee!—that is, if they didn't forego the pretensions and simply have at the fifty-pound sack of sunflower seeds: chew through the paper wrap and gorge themselves in a roly-poly Roman sort of mockery.

Willoughby, fed up with all this coarseness and gluttony, while her cinnamon bun was warming in the microwave oven, dashed out on the porch in her flannel pajamas and army jacket, packing the BB pistol that had become her weapon of choice in her campaign against the squirrels. Seconds later, the microwave oven beeped in the kitchen and the morning peace was shattered by a horrendous wail.

You talk about a scream to wake the dead! Jed sat bolt upright in bed, staring at the walls of his room, his heart ricocheting so loudly off his ribs that Dmitri, hearing that preternatural beat, leaped off the foot of the bed, arched his back and hissed at him.

Jed scrambled out of bed and down the stairs, sped through the kitchen on his mother's and grandfather's heels, and raced outside to the porch, all three of them fearing that Willoughby had met with some awful calamity.

"Willoughby!"

The grass was clumped with dew where Willoughby stood barefoot in her flannel pajamas and drab army jacket. In her hand the BB pistol was still raised toward Jupiter. At her feet a red squirrel crawled in the grass, or rather dragged itself inch by excruciating inch, making woefully slow progress, most of the way writhing on its side and twisting uncontrollably, its limp tail beating in the grass. A look of melancholy repulsion had settled on Willoughby's face. Her mouth bore traces of the blue lipstick a Nordstrom cosmetician had applied to it yesterday morning in Anchorage.

"Do something," she begged Jed, throwing the gun down in front of him. "Can't you do something?"

It was all right for Willoughby, she was an early riser. Jed wouldn't normally have risen for school for another hour. By the time he had gone to bed last night, after seeing to his trap, it was well past midnight, and so he hardly felt indebted to Willoughby for her waking him at this early hour for *this* ungodly disaster.

"Like do what?"

"Anything!"

For reasons that would later bear thinking about, Jed's sister and mother and grandfather all looked to him to do something for the unfortunate squirrel. The squirrel soon died and there wasn't much that could be done for it. Jed reasoned that a BB had pierced its eye and penetrated to its brain, hence the weird convulsions and the untimely but merciful death that followed. He carried the little corpse to the edge of the woods and left it under a vault of withered cranberries.

A freak accident, he explained to the family. But they needn't have worried about the trauma to Willoughby's emotions. What befell the squirrel didn't hit her nearly as hard as the collapse of her Beach Buggy two days earlier. On Monday afternoon, home from school, Willoughby appeared to have forgotten all about the squirrel. Her weekend in Anchorage had done her a world of good.

"The Holiday Inn was pretty cool," she said. "They gave our room away by mistake, so we got to stay in a suite for free. Remember the pool? They totally fixed it up."

She was bubbly and talkative, following Jed around the chicken house. He was taking advantage of the sunshine to sweep the coop floor and to lay down fresh sawdust.

"You should see Mom's boobs," she said. "They're like totally huge. All those blue veins in them. It looks like Rockford cheese. I know what she got for your present. We went to a million stores, shopping for stuff."

"Almond Roca?"

"Warm."

"Marzipan?"

"Maybe."

"Night-vision goggles?"

"You wish."

Businesslike robins patrolled the lawn, dwarfing the little finches. The robins only visited the Hanson place in fair weather. Monday evening was so mild that Jed and Grandpa Henry grilled salmon steaks outside. It was their first barbecue of the year.

While they tended the steaks, basting and turning them, the chickens ranged and bobbed in the grass at their feet. Jed was eager to tell Grandpa Henry of the fox's making off with the grouse wing last night. Although he knew it was superstitious of him to say so, he wondered aloud if the fox trap had been an unlucky one. "Some trappers throw away the first trap every season."

"Nothing wrong with being a little superstitious," Grandpa said.

"I'll set one of the other traps," Jed said.

"Some things are what you believe them to be. I had a wart on my finger when I was your age. My grandfather—I loved him very much, God bless him—Granddad told me to cut a potato in half and rub it on my wart and then bury it outside."

"Did it work?"

"I don't know if it worked, Jed, but the wart was gone in two days."

"Wow."

Jed watched Grandpa Henry brushing the honey sauce on the salmon steaks. Since his fall yesterday, Grandpa had been plagued by stomach pains and bouts of dizziness. Mrs. Hanson had made an appointment for him to see one of the local oncologists.

"I sometimes wonder," Grandpa went on, "if I would have this doggone arthritis in my leg if I had worn copper bracelets on my wrist and ankle the way Granddad did. My grandfather was a skeptical man, but once he put his faith on the table, you couldn't argue with it. He never had arthritis that I knew of."

Jed listened with pleasure to his grandfather's accounts of superstitions that had been vindicated, but in his heart of hearts he knew better than to believe that a metal contraption like a fox trap could be unlucky in itself. Rusty, maybe; man-smelling, maybe;

but unlucky? No, if any superstition had dawned in Jed, it had grown out of something entirely different, out of the animal spirits of the living fox, and that was something harder to explain.

But...there was a moment last night when the fox seemed to have been transformed into a winged creature. Obviously, feathers didn't sprout from its withers, nothing as outlandish as that, winged foxes have been extinct for at least five hundred years, but...he was such a fine fox to look at, so handsome, so lithe, so prudent and sharp, he inhabited his body with such superb facility that he seemed to Jed at that moment to soar toward some life's zenith where his fox's form became irrelevant and it was just the stuff and force of his being alive that mattered. All the edges of Jed's body prickled with wakefulness afterwards when he lay in bed thinking about it. In his mind he kept seeing the fox rearing on the earthen bank, leaping across the hollow, and vanishing into the woods with the grouse wing clasped in his mouth. Had the fox known Jed was watching? Known and defied him anyway?

But you couldn't know what a fox was thinking. You could only watch him and learn by watching. This was not the same as science, not exactly. *"The difference between biology and science, between animal behavior as I study it, and the scientific method, is the difference between life and death."* With these words Mr. Hanson had explained his work to Jed's fifth-grade class on Parent Teaching Day three years ago. *"I'm a wildlife biologist first, a scientist second."* Yes, you had to allow for the animal spirits. You had to develop your own kind of stealth, your own instinct, your own fox luck.

The Hanson women held a fashion show that night after supper. They modeled their purchases from their recent Anchorage expedition, passing before the table where Jed and Grandpa Henry sat eating toffees from the box of them that Mrs. Hanson had bought as a gift for Jed.

"I loaned out all my maternity clothes after Jed was born, and of course that was the end of that," Mrs. Hanson said. "I never saw them again. Not that I had very many. You can see why," she added, using a pair of nail clippers to snip a price tag off one of the new garments. "But I'm not being fair, I must have given them away for keeps. I never dreamed I'd need them again. Lord, it's probably the only time I'll fit clothes I wore fourteen years ago."

The new maternity suits were puzzling in the extreme. They came with expanding flaps and elastic cords, adjustable waistlines and secret windows through which the wearer could nurse an infant. Willoughby and Mrs. Hanson put their heads together to solve the workings of each garment.

"You had it right yesterday, Mom."

"This isn't it?"

"Duh. That's where your arm goes."

Grandpa Henry, who wore sweaters even back home in California—he chilled easily, on account of his sluggish circulation—was given a lovely cardigan of qiviut wool for his present. Willoughby meanwhile did numerous encores in her stylish two-piece suit of black denim, and she was proud beyond words of her new pair of pointy-toed, lace-up black boots, footwear which her mother looked askance at as the sort of boots ladies of the night used to wear in the days of Jack the Ripper.

But the highlight of the fashion show was a kind of rude corset or stretchable girdle that Mrs. Hanson stepped into and worked up around her waist. The device was supposed to reduce the physical burden to her of carrying a child by relieving the strain to her back and belly. "The salesgirl swore by it," Mrs. Hanson grunted as she tugged at the webbing that enclosed her, "but I never tried one of these before. I don't know. She said I'd be glad I bought it."

With her skirt overflowing her arms, Mrs. Hanson cinched the broad belt high on her belly, muttering that she felt like a horse in it. Her family said nothing to confirm or deny the impression. There may have been a suppressed titter from Jed or Willoughby, but they otherwise refrained from clapping or commenting and let their silence be the measure of their tribute.

Alaska is a creature of its latitudes and seasons. In the interior of the state in May, you can read a book in the window until late at night without having to rely on any lamplight. The summer solstice was little more than a month away. "It is hard to believe, hard to believe,"

Fairbanksans muttered, and the thing which they muttered about was the speed with which life seemed to move along.

Jed, endlessly fascinated by the adventures of Roy Chapman Andrews, had read so far in his book tonight that he dreaded its inevitable end. Imagine exploring the Gobi Desert for dinosaur eggs! You're bound to push as far afield as Mr. Andrews if you're ever going to find anything as worthwhile in life as dinosaur eggs. Jed would receive science credit for reading the biography, and that was a good thing because, for as long as the book lasted, he could honestly say he was staying up late to do his homework.

And so he read by the light of the picture window, with his binoculars at hand—keeping a lookout for the fox—and after several hours had gone by, sometime after midnight but before cockcrow, his mother found him there, asleep at the table. He had baited a fresh trap that evening, using salmon scraps gleaned from the family's supper plates, but no matter how fresh the trap or fragrant the bait, the fox didn't come that night.

In his bedroom Jed lay reproaching himself for having slept at all. It sometimes happens, when your fatigue gets the better of you and you're too excited to sleep, that your mind becomes relentlessly active, even agitated. Such a process may have explained why Jed with the passing minutes became convinced that at any second he would hear a blood-curdling scream. He heard the scream gathering in his mind's ear; he listened for it, believing it was pointless to sleep when the scream would only wake him; and since the scream never came, it was always a heart's beat from doing so.

To pass the night in this way would have become tedious except for the happy coincidence that Jed was at the same moment setting out on an expedition into the Gobi Desert—and in very prestigious company, too. What fun! The merciless sun beating down on them, the camels spitting and swishing their tails, Mr. Chapman Andrews heaved to beside Jed's camel and invited Jed to take some refreshments in his tent, there was the matter of the fossilized remains of the blue-haired bladderolypus he wished to consult him on...

Jed heard footsteps in the house and laughed into his pillow, musing how both his mother and his grand-father visited the bathroom at all hours of the night, though of course for very different reasons. Ha, ha! It seemed nobody slept in the Hanson house anymore.

His mind careened from thought to thought in this way and toward morning he became quite feverish. When he closed his eyes, the dome of his skull lit up with wild phantasms; monsters from an old bestiary paraded there; fuzzy protozoans swam the gray seas of his consciousness; suddenly the shrieks pierced his hearing, his heart pounded for the tribulations of a dying rabbit, and it didn't matter how forcefully he squeezed his eyes shut, his mind only thrived, rampant with visions of the world in infrared.

This exceptional psychic condition, these nervous disturbances persisted in Jed for the rest of the night and throughout Tuesday's waking hours. The less he slept and the more his imagination rampaged, the more he enjoyed himself, or imagined he did. After several nights of insufficient sleep, Jed didn't know how exhausted he was, and so it came as a surprise to him, though perhaps it shouldn't have, to learn from his mother, on Tuesday after school, that both the school nurse and the algebra teacher had phoned her to notify her that Jed had fallen asleep in his chair in class.

"I did?"

Strictly speaking, it was illegal to trap a fox in May. It may not have been wrong, but it was unlawful, and so Jed had avoided telling his school friends about a matter in which they would otherwise have taken the warmest interest. The relief that comes from sharing a preoccupation with a sympathetic friend was therefore denied to him, and since his preoccupation had only itself to grow on, it lost its due proportion as one of many elements in his life.

"Yes, you did," his mother ripped back at him. "Don't be a smart aleck."

But for Jed the only functioning circuit of his mind was this one of the fox and chickens. There was the fox and the unfinished matter of trapping it: every other thought petered out in the fog of his exhaustion. Shouldn't he be pleased that the fox had stayed away on Monday night? Wasn't that the idea? That the fox should not trespass? Not menace his chickens? And yet he looked forward to the fox's return. Everything had flip-flopped. His obligation to trap the fox had become an unmet challenge: the chickens were the chore now, the fox what compelled him.

"You're to be in bed at eight o'clock tonight, no ifs, ands, or buts about it."

"Eight o'clock!"

"Bait your trap and go to bed. You don't need to stay up."

"But I do, it's not the same."

"Trappers don't wait around watching their traps. Just look at you, you're like an ape with your mouth hanging open."

"He always looks like that," Willoughby interjected.

"That's enough, Willoughby, you're not much better," Mrs. Hanson said.

"I don't eat a whole box of toffees to keep me up at night, if that's what you mean," Willoughby said.

"It wasn't a whole box, not after you got done with it," Jed said.

"'Listless, lethargic, inattentive,'" Mrs. Hanson quoted the school nurse. "'Nervous. Abstracted.' And a temperature, too."

"Not!" Jed was outraged. The nurse had exaggerated. "I'm fine, I swear I am." A fraudulent liveliness entered his manner. It drained all his energy just to follow the argument. He was hot behind the temples, his nose and ears were plugged up.

"I happen to know you've been wearing the same underwear for three days in a row," his mother said.

"Yuk," Willoughby cried. "Gross!"

"Get lost, Willoughby," Jed yelled.

"If it comes to a choice between your schoolwork and your chickens, the chickens will have to go, Jed, do you understand?"

"Uh-huh."

"Your falling asleep in class doesn't reflect well on me."

"I didn't mean to embarrass you," Jed said.

"I have many things to worry about. I want you both to keep quiet tonight. Grandpa's appointment's tomorrow and he needs his rest."

Grandpa Henry had stayed in bed all day and Jed hadn't seen him since getting home from school that afternoon. He hadn't been more than usually concerned for the old man until now, seeing his mother as grim as she was.

"Is he feeling bad?"

"Is he feeling bad?" Willoughby mimicked her brother and ended with a snort. "God, what a dope."

"Hey, you know, I'm just about sick of you," Jed said. "I'm not five years old anymore."

"Stop it," Mrs. Hanson said.

"Fat maggot," Jed said.

"Why don't you tell him," Willoughby said. "Doesn't he know?"

"Know what?" Jed said.

"He's dying, you idiot."

"Willoughby!"

"He's not dying," Jed said.

"Of course he's dying," Willoughby cried, "why do you think he's here? To see a moose? Why would anyone come to Fairbanks except to die!"

If it was true that Jed, in an earlier moment of astonishment, had resembled an ape, he was now in the company of his mother, who stood speechless in the face of Willoughby's onslaught.

Mrs. Hanson's voice, when she spoke, was barely audible. "I think you need to go to your room, Willoughby."

"For what? Telling the truth?"

"For the way you tell it."

"Why does everyone pretend? Pretend pretend pretend! That's all you do! Pretend!"

The discussion had begun as a gentle warning to Jed, and here was Willoughby in a budding rage again. Willoughby had backed away and stood in a self-protective posture, her head drawn down and her side turned toward them. The atmosphere of accusation and hurt was too unbearable to be sustained, and, so that Willoughby should not be the first to run away, as she appeared on the verge of doing, Mrs. Hanson quickly turned and strode from the room, dispirited and lacking the will to battle any further with her children.

4

Now, this thing about death, about dying. What could he do? Why does it happen so often the unintended end of our actions is another death? There was the time four years ago when he was forced to put to sleep—to put out of her misery—his pet cat Delilah. His father wouldn't let him take her to the pound, arguing that Jed must learn "responsibility." Now the memory reawakened all the bitter heartache of that time. He had started with a beautiful cat and he ended by burying her.

Birds brain themselves on the picture window; voles drown in derelict buckets; the BB pistol takes its gruesome toll. Do we control these bloody outbreaks? We seem to be predators without even preying. Wherever we set ourselves up in the world, there's an interface of death, where the birds fly into our windows and the voles fall into our buckets. How sad!

One fine spring day Jed brings home Blind Boy and twenty-nine other chicks from the feed store, little knowing he's bringing five of them to an early doom. For that matter, Blind Boy wasn't Blind Boy to begin with. What cruelty in the way of things causes a flock of chickens to turn on one of their own and peck his eye out?

And the war! God! More than sixty million people! *Pfft. Schwipf.* Just like that. Jed had looked it up in the encyclopedia after Grandpa Henry spoke of it. How many at the Battle of the Bulge alone! Nineteen thousand of ours, not to mention the captured and wounded. That's why Grandpa Henry was needed—as a replacement, because tens of thousands of soldiers were maimed and killed before him at the Bulge and young Henry might just have to go next. Yes, and then Grandma, a designer at Douglas Aircraft when she met Grandpa, would never have had a daughter and Jed wouldn't be here in the middle of the night to consider his nonexistence!

This is what you get for going to bed early, he thought. It was three o'clock in the morning. The irony being that it wasn't from restlessness that he couldn't sleep, but because he had already slept seven hours. She had been so cross, his mother, he hadn't wanted to cross her further by arguing about his bedtime, and the truth of the matter was, he had been exhausted last night, so exhausted he barely had the strength to burrow under the sheets.

He and Willoughby had made it up after their fight. "You're not a maggot." "You're not a dope." They were quits. She suggested that he sneak into her room after their mother went to bed, he could keep his vigil over the chicken coop from her window. Jed agreed to the scheme but failed to stay awake for it.

And so he lay with his hands folded under his head, revolving his thoughts at leisure. He felt clear-minded now. For two days his brain had been the hot center of a galaxy of wild impressions. It was as though the fox world and the man world had collided in him and their approach to each other had disordered his senses. He certainly had carried on about it. Like a headless chicken!

It wouldn't have happened that way if Mr. Hanson were still alive. No, Jed had an inkling what his father would say. *There's no getting around having to trap the fox, Jed. Don't worry, the earth isn't going to quake about it. By the way, there's no collision of the fox world and the man world because they're one and the same creation. Or haven't you studied geometry yet. Stay in tune. If you've got a problem, take care of it.*

Oh, yes. Jed's mouth turned up in a smile when he remembered what a reasonable man his father had been.

And it was true. Jed wouldn't alter a thing by trapping the fox, not really. In theory the scientists, armed with their high-sounding commissions, could one day exterminate wild foxes and introduce in their place a species cured of its taste for poultry. But the principle doesn't change. One day it might be wild kangaroos preying on your chickens, you never know. Don't forget, wild horses and tigers once roamed Alaska's grasslands.

In Jed's case it was a matter of choosing between the fox and his chickens. He was neither a destroyer nor avenger, and it was perfectly natural that the fox had eaten his chickens.

People will still thrill to mayhem at the movies. Drink hot cocoa in the morning. You leave a bucket outside, the bucket catches rain, foolish voles go swimming, magpies rejoice.

There seemed to be no way out of it. Any way you turned, something had to give; something suffered, something died, and so much of the world is raised on a leaven of anguish not our own.

"Jed."

"Huh?"

Jed turned in his bed, looking toward the door. His grandfather's voice, no longer that of a hale man, came as a ghostly rustle.

"Grandpa?"

Henry's tall figure loomed in the doorway. "Do you want to get out of bed? I think I saw him out there."

Jed threw back his blanket. "The fox?"

"I believe it is. Kind of stealing down in the yard. Only saw him from the window, I was coming back from the men's room."

"Thanks, Grandpa. Come on," Jed whispered.

The forest, or the stretch of forest visible to them from the picture window, was backed by a pale rectangular light, the clearing of the roadbed in the distance. Against this light the trees stood outlined, here joining in a mass of deep shadow where the heavy boughs sagged over the forest floor, and there raising their slender tops in a spray of curling branches.

The morning was dim, but by degrees became less so. The garage had lost its menacing shape and assumed a gentler appearance, and beyond it, tucked like a hobbit's house at the edge of the woods, was the chicken coop. The sight of the boxy little shelter in the shadow of the woods stirred Jed's heart. And just beyond the chicken coop, the fox trap was set at the foot of the grizzled birch tree.

The undergrowth is light in May, the roses and cranberries thin, the horsetails bare shoots. The cover was sparse and didn't conceal the white flash of the fox's tail as he made his way toward the birch tree.

Jed leaned across the table, pressing his binoculars close, his pulse pattering insistently in his fingertips. A full minute passed, and then another as the fox sidled in toward the birch tree, approaching from the far side as he had done in the past.

The fox crept under the slanting trunk of the birch tree and onto the hump of earth and leaves at its base.

He stood his forelegs on this rim of earthbound roots and peered into the hollow below.

Jed had baited the fox trap as before, by baiting the hole he had dug in the earth, but, in addition—the only thing he had done differently this time—he had tossed a salmon skin into the hollow and left it there for the fox to get wind of. He didn't bury the scrap, he didn't hide it deep in the hollow, no, he just dropped it on the ground as a sloppy human being would do, something a shrewd fox like this was sure to understand and believe in.

And the fox glanced toward the house, he nosed the air, he looked down in the hollow at the scrap of salmon skin. He nosed the air, he glanced toward the house, he lowered his head over the fish scrap and took it.

The fox retreated a few steps and ate the fish, wolfing it down with full movements of his head, the way a dog dramatically devours a treat you have given him. And both Jed and the fox were confident now: Jed that if the fox returned for seconds he would step where he shouldn't, and the fox that he wanted more of this tasty meal so easily come by.

And so he rounded the trunk again and stretched forth his neck, nuzzling over the hollow. There had never been a trap here, not in this fox's experience. And this was a fox of foxes, lean with pains taken and canny with lessons learned. And so, after the slightest hesitation, he stepped down in the hollow and trod lightly in a circle, then very suddenly he jumped a tail's length in the air.

The silence, when you are watching through binoculars, is unrelated to what you are actually seeing, and that's the strange and disconcerting thing about it. Jed didn't hear the jaws spring shut, the chain rattle, or the leaves get beaten up. Silence was the context for all of it.

"Well, that's that," Grandpa said.

Jed put his binoculars down and went for his clothes and his rifle.

The fox, when he saw Jed coming down the yard, renewed his fight to escape the leghold, jerking his hind leg and tugging against it. But that struggle soon ended, and he stood at his ease and watched Jed come on.

Jed was of the opinion—it was only an opinion—that the fox understood everything that had happened to it, and everything that was going to happen, understood it in whatever way it is that a fox understands. There was a look of hard-won wisdom on the animal's face. Jed put the muzzle on his forehead and the fox died right away.

He liked to think of it as forgiveness, but whatever it was that Jed needed, he obtained it in a murmured exchange with the fox, or, if you'd rather, with his own conscience. Then he freed the fox from the trap and carried it into the garage, where he hung it by a hind leg from a wire gambrel and switched on a light he could work by.

And Jed spent the hours until dawn, and, it turned out, most of Wednesday, skinning and fleshing the fox, as he was a fine fox and Jed owed him full honors. He performed this duty with the utmost care, guiding his knife so as not to puncture the fox skin, and his concentration was such that he lost all track of the time. He had loosened the pelt as far down as the fox's belly, and had just reached up to free the end of it from its attachment to the tail bone, when his mother tapped at the open door of the garage and looked in on him.

"Grandpa said I'd find you here. Willoughby's got band practice an hour before first bell. I've got to drop her off. There's breakfast on the stove."

His hands were bloody and he kept them clear of his mother as she hugged him. He showed her the slip-joint pliers he was using to strip the tail bone from the fox pelt. "Dad taught me this trick," he said.

"Well, I hope on Thursday you'll apply all this ingenuity at school."

"You mean I can skip today?"

"It looks like you'll have to."

Jed nodded. "He's a nice fox."

"I shouldn't lose my temper the way I did last night, Jed. I'm sorry."

"That's okay."

There was something else his mother wished to speak to him about, Jed could tell it by her hesitation, but Willoughby was already yelling at them from the driveway, blaring on her trombone to hurry things up. "I'll be late!"

"My keys," Mrs. Hanson said. And she dashed off to find her purse. "Grandpa's doctor appointment's today, he's coming with us," she called back. "Bring my rose out in the sun, please. And eat some breakfast!"

Jed worked steadily in the garage till midmorning, and without stopping for lunch he carried his tools outside and resumed his task in the sun. And that's where his family found him hours later, seated in the sunlight in front of the chicken coop, using a scraper to flesh the fat off the fox pelt, which he had stretched on a smooth board in front of him while the chickens traipsed in the grass at his feet.

"Their liberator," Willoughby said.

And what word from Grandpa Henry's doctor?

"He told me to go home and have a barbecue," Grandpa said.

"He did?"

"He did."

"We'll see if I don't have the patties ready before Grandpa gets the coals done," Mrs. Hanson challenged them and started for the house.

"Two barbecues in one week," Jed said.

"Summer's here," Willoughby cried. "Yahooo!"

Jed shooed a fly off the fox pelt and rose to help Grandpa Henry at the barbecue. It may have been summer for the young people, but Grandpa Henry, always sensitive to a chill, was wearing his new sweater, the cardigan they had bought him in Anchorage.

"That's all the doctor said?" Jed asked him.

"He gave me some pills for the dizziness."

"Do they work?"

"Sure, they work."

Jed didn't know what else to ask Henry, or not to ask him, or how directly to ask him about his cancer, and so he fumbled for words.

Grandpa Henry chuckled at something or other.

"Speaking of fainting fits," he said, "that tree there looks about ready to keel over."

Jed laughed too, nodding at the old birch tree. "I don't think so. It always tips like that." He pointed to where the birch trunk slanted up from the earth. "Willoughby used to climb up there and we'd wrestle on it. Mom always told Dad to cut it down, she was afraid it would fall on us."

"I can see why she worried."

"Nah. She was just jealous he was always raking the leaves up."

Grandpa Henry laughed merrily at that. "A husband will hear about it."

"Want to see something, Grandpa?" Jed stepped back and squinted at him.

"Like what, Jed?"

"Come on, I'll show you."

The coals were mounded in the barbecue, the orange flames spreading across them. Jed glanced at Willoughby in the driveway. The trunk of the car was open and she was throwing the remnants of her Beach Buggy into it, for taking to the dump later.

"It's from twenty years ago," Jed said, leading his grandfather around the birch tree to where a slim reddish branch grew off the trunk at eye level. A tone of awe had entered Jed's voice. He nudged Grandpa's arm. "Look."

There, in the node where the branch joined the main trunk of the tree, the remains of an old cant hook hung embedded. The curved blade of the tool had hung for such a long time in this spot—for the twenty years since Mr. Hanson had built the house—that the tree had incorporated the blade into itself, its wood swelled and grown around the metal and sealed it there.

"He used it for moving logs with, that's what it's for," Jed said.

The exposed blade, or the part of it not buried in the flesh of the tree, had rusted brown. The wooden handle was gray and weathered, what remained of it.

Grandpa Henry moved his trembling fingers over the skin of the birch tree, where it had stretched around the tool, enclosing it.

"Look at that," Henry whispered.

And Jed nodded his head knowingly. Not for the first time, he imagined his father as he might have appeared twenty years ago, young Mr. Hanson hanging that cant hook in the birch tree one day after laying the last round of logs on the house walls—*Oh, yeah!*—just striding by and swinging it there: it was a kingly gesture every time Jed conjured it.

The growth of green was phenomenal that year. The green of the grass, the dark green of the spruce trees, the chokecherry leaves light green in the sun, the dazzling greens of the birches—it was a play of greens, one upon the other, and in the rain the leaves glowed with a rich green luster.

The town of Fairbanks boasts its share, possibly more than its share, of cranks and sourpusses, but there is not an icy heart among them that doesn't melt when the first dandelion raises its golden head in the grass. Next come the bluebells and the wild roses, enlivening the roadsides and pocketing the woods with shades of pink and blue. In summer the tourists flock to the town which at other times of the year they would gladly consign to the chillier regions of hell. The residents, taking their cue from the butterflies, fly up and down their lists of activities. They fish, they build, they trade, they grow, they prosper. It is another Fairbanks summer and nobody stops living for even a minute.

Dmitri the housecat goes three quarters wild and disappears for days at a time. Mrs. Hanson works like mad in her flower and vegetable garden. Grandpa Henry keeps fit by helping her, and indeed Grandpa Henry has moved into the Hanson house for good.

Grandpa's move was made official on that memorable evening in May after Jed had trapped the red fox. It was the night of the famous barbecue at which Jed and Willoughby devoured the better part of six cheeseburgers and ramrodded them down with eleven dill pickles. The lengthening days had lengthened their appetites, you might say, and they slopped everything on those burgers they could think of.

After the banquet Mrs. Hanson made two family announcements. The first concerned this matter of

Grandpa Henry's moving in with them. "Your grand-father and I have talked it over," she explained to the children, "and if it's all right with you two, he's decided to sell his California house and come live with us."

Well! The new arrangement would require adjust-ments in the family routine, but these were gladly con-sented to by Jed and Willoughby, who had gotten so used to Grandpa Henry and his wise and dependable company, it was as if he had always been there with them.

"And there is something else," Mrs. Hanson said. "This isn't going to be as easy for me." She studied her hands in silence before looking around at the faces of her family. "I think you all know who Mr. Allen is."

At this, the children started in their chairs and traded meaningful glances. This was not going to be the usual table talk.

"In Anchorage," their mother went on, "Willoughby was at my throat non-stop about Mr. Allen. She was merciless. Mr. Allen this, Mr. Allen that. I tried not to be upset. I don't know how you kids figured it out, but you did.

"In plain words...well, it isn't easy for me to say this, but after your father died, and after some time passed, I became very lonely. Mr. Allen and I had what you might call a love affair. And until yesterday I thought, I even hoped, it might be more than that. But, until yes-terday, I had never demanded a decision from him— about the future, I mean. I put that off. And I put it off because...I must have known what his answer would be.

"Mr. Allen has a peculiar sense of humor." And here some recollection associated with her words brought tears to Mrs. Hanson's eyes. "I liked that most of all about him. But I didn't know how implacable it could be. He thinks that having children is a tragedy. He doesn't want to build a life with me, with us, as this child's father, and it's that simple.

"As painful as it was for me to hear this, it was necessary. And it wasn't fair of me to draw it out, it wasn't fair to you kids, I saw that. Whatever pain I felt, it was wrong of me to come home in a temper and take it out on you. I'm sorry.

"The bonds that hold us together have to be real bonds. I would never in a million years want to hold Mr. Allen against his will, even if I could do that. But I'm not going to sit here and say this child was a mistake, not at all. Don't let me or anyone else ever give you that idea. I am going to have this child, we're going to have it together, all of us, we'll go through this together and see it as the beginning that it is, and keep getting on and on with our lives."

And the story might have ended there, except that the story never does. It happened early one morning, almost a month later, that a red fox came trotting across the Hanson yard, and Jed was able to watch her from the picture window.

She was a smaller, more slender fox than the fox which he had trapped, and in fact she was traveling on the first fox's trail. Of this Jed was certain, for the reason that when, lowering her nose, she came to the base of the old birch tree, where the scent and its trail ended together, she abruptly stopped and stood there, alone and plainly bewildered.

The trail had led her to this place and then it led nowhere at all. It made no sense to her. She glanced around at the lawn and the forest, as if considering which path to take next, and after a while she turned and trotted away in the direction she had come from.

The forest understory was deep now. The horse-tails had grown tall, the cranberries filled out. She must have kits at home that needed minding. Those kits would be about the age of Jed's chickens, come to think of it. The bereaved fox returned once more a few days later, and then Jed didn't see her again.

Somehow, you thought that the process would stop or slow or alter, but it never does. Memories turn through the mind, but memory lives in the top of the chest, the base of the throat. Jed stood outside where the she-fox had stood, and he gazed after her, to see what she might have seen. The spruce tops lorded over him, somber and fatherly and full of comfort to him.

Mrs. Hanson went in for routine blood tests. The doctors were frank with her. She wasn't exactly a spring chicken anymore and they wanted to know of any antibodies in her blood that discouraged breast feeding. But everything checked out fine. In her belly the baby was almost a foot tall.

Grandpa Henry had blood tests too. The doctors sent to California for his medical records and they entered the battle against his disease with all the vigor and vitality of the season.

And Jed's chickens? They had no more visits from predators that summer. They roamed in the grass, foraging for seeds and nabbing mosquitos from the air. They ate with such monstrous appetites, they consumed so much food and grew so fast, that they soon became extremely ungainly, and for Jed it wasn't always easy to associate these lumbering giants with the fuzzy red and yellow chicks he had brought home from the feed store two months before.

The chickens, for their part, adored Jed. Their "liberator," as Willoughby called him. They flocked at his heels, happily clucking when he fed and watered them. But some things don't change, and at roundup time they turned their backs and fled from him, upbraiding him and colliding with one another and proving as agile as ever in eluding his warm clutches.

Of Knives and Men

Why I had agreed to help slaughter and butcher twenty sheep when I had never in my life so much as peeked into the sack of giblets that comes with a store-bought chicken, and why I laid down fifty dollars to become the proud owner of one of these doomed animals when the taste of lamb repels me—these were questions I might have been expected to ask myself, and my wife asked me these very questions as I donned my longjohns after breakfast. I darted outside without answering her because Merry is one of those women whose sportive smiles make a man feel he is ever on the verge of foolishness.

The sheep congregated inside the corral, humped, pale and softly bleating in the dawn. My neighbor Steve and his father Ernie crunched toward me through the frosted pasture, Steve shouldering his .22 rifle. Yesterday we had chalked orange Xs on the haunches of the sheep we wanted. It was late September and cold and we watched them through our rising breaths.

I was new to Alaska, and when a man comes to Alaska he is liable to undertake any number of extravagant deeds to measure up to the glorious traditions of the sourdoughs. Ernie himself was a preeminent sourdough, a huge man with a gentle smile, a pot belly, a head of snowy hair and a black Machinists Union jacket. He had piloted a B-17 during World War II and a Super Cub in the Alaska Range. He had done stints in the timber and cannery industries. He had trapped, barged, prospected, delivered mail by dogsled, and operated a summer trading post on the Noatak. Also worked as an Alaska Railroad conductor and a camp manager during construction of the Pipeline. He still ran a placer mine in the Interior. Did I forget commercial fisherman? To a greenhorn like myself, Ernie was as big as all Alaska, and I knew I could trust him to shepherd us through the task that lay ahead.

I wanted to put some meat by for the winter, for myself and for Merry and for the child in her womb. We would have lamb burgers this winter, lamb with wild cranberries, and ground lamb lasagna. Meat is meat, and it didn't matter at all, in the beautiful hungry scheme of things, that the taste of lamb is something I cannot stand.

At the borders of the pasture, the spruce tops pointed dark and furred against the blue morning sky. Simon the ram, tethered alone in the pasture, repeatedly charged us as we lingered between him and the corral. Every charge ended the same way, with Simon coming chockablock to the end of his rope and suffering a whiplash that left him coughing and staggering. That didn't stop him from circling and lowering his head for another charge.

The lambs spooked and bleated when we entered the corral. Before long we had cornered one of the marked creatures and wrestled it out of the gate, and its fleece warmed my hands as we carry-pulled it up to the edge of the spruce woods, where Steve had erected a crossbar and tied a red flag to it to warn any passerby that this was a place of slaughter.

We flipped the bucking lamb over on a square of plywood and argued whether to shoot the animal or to cut its throat. Dung was clinging to its stubby tail. As Steve had his .22 rifle handy, he was naturally inclined to use it, so, tall and skinny like something that grew quickly one arctic summer and never had a chance to grow sideways, Steve, in his old green service jacket, pressed the muzzle of his rifle to the lamb's forehead and without delay pulled the trigger. We knotted short lengths of rope around the lamb's hind legs, hoisted the carcass and tied it to the crossbar.

Well, our lamb was no sooner hanging upside-down from the crossbar than it opened its eyes and looked around at us. It was a piteous sight. We hardly had time to be perplexed by this development before Merry arrived from the house with a bucket of hot water. "You'll need water to clean your knives," she said, and I didn't wait before gratefully plunging my cold hands into the bucket.

Steve did likewise, but Ernie, the old gentleman, remained standing between my wife and the resuscitated lamb. I was reminded of the time Steve's wife Becky, who had run off two months earlier, set the corner of their house on fire with a weed burner and tried to hide it from Steve by standing in front of the flames. Merry stepped around Ernie and stared at the lamb as it swung to and fro and blinked its eyes at us.

"It's still alive," she said.

"Well, we've got to bleed it," Ernie explained. He thoughtfully rubbed his jaw. "We've got to bleed it while the heart is beating."

"Of course it's alive," Steve said. He and I stepped closer and examined the lamb. "But it's unconscious."

"Don't tell me that animal's unconscious," Merry said.

I scrutinized the lamb, wrinkling my forehead in my effort, and sure enough that lamb was blinking and quietly trembling. "Steve," I declared, "this animal is conscious."

"I just shot it with the rifle," he protested.

"The shot went crooked," I said. No one was pulling anything over on my wife, I gladly realized, but not wanting to get into a discussion of the relative pain and suffering of this animal, I gave Merry a pointed look.

"Well, don't just stand there," she said.

I glanced at Steve and Ernie, but clearly neither one of them was prepared to perform the actual act in front of my wife, a beautiful black-haired woman in a red plaid Pendleton, so I in a fit of pique picked up the nearest knife and, clenching my jaws, pushed the blade into the lamb's throat. The blade met some resistance, so I dropped the knife and took up another, and I will never forget the lesson I learned that morning of the consequences of not sharpening your knives when you ought.

Three grown men might have butchered, barbecued and digested five sheep in the time it took us to disassemble this one. Since I was already cutting the sheep's neck, it naturally fell to me to remove the whole head, so there I squatted, sawing with a knife no sharper than a fiddle bow while Steve and Ernie worked above me on the hocks, softly cursing as their dull knives tangled in the fleece.

"Did you see that?" Merry said.

"That's just reflex," Ernie said.

"It kicked."

"Don't get upset," he repeated. "Reflex."

I wasn't so sure. Under the impression that moist breath was emanating from the lamb's mouth, I desperately manipulated the knife. It had finally dawned on Steve and Ernie and me that Merry was not going back to the house, and although I tried not to resent her intrusion, I couldn't help entertaining mean thoughts like—Woman, why don't you go home and read a magazine. But she laughed at me (I'd wrapped my arms around the sheep's head in an effort to detach it by force) and my wife's laughter always softens my heart. The sheep's head twisted off and Steve and Ernie laughed too as I fell on my hindquarters with the whole curly noggin in my lap.

The day was warmer. The mist had lifted from the woods, and the sight of camp robbers landing around us and stealing the bits of fat that we had flung off our knives lifted my spirits, camp robbers being welcome players in the beautiful hungry scheme of things.

"Cut these sinews," Ernie told Merry, guiding her hand on the knife, "you don't want to puncture the skin, but you don't want to puncture the gut, either."

Merry glanced at me, pleased to be helping, her cheeks brightly flushed, and I nearly yelled with the giddy joy of it, certain that I would come to love the taste of lamb this winter, and looking forward to those long nights and smoke smells and parading silver moons with just me and Merry under our high cathedral ceiling squeezing each other unto April which seemed as good a month as any to have a child born in, planned or not. There she stood in her red plaid Pendleton with sheep blood dripping on her boots, learning from this kindly old sourdough who wore a hearing aid because he had worked with loud machines all his life, and she looked so beautiful that I decided that tonight when this was over I would ask her into the spruce woods for a real lovers' walk.

I couldn't blame Steve for not sharing my happiness at that moment, his Becky having abandoned him so recently, but I nearly shinned him with my steel-toed boot when he did what he did.

Merry and Ernie had stripped off most of the sheep's skin and Ernie was describing to her how cuddlesome the skin would be after tanning when Steve became impatient with their chatter and took it on himself to snip the animal's belly lengthwise, causing a distinctive odor to be released—not his own, I mean, but the sheep's. The pungent fecal gut smell caught Merry off guard and sent her eyeballs kind of rolling up in her head.

Merry reeled and dropped her arms to her sides, and I, desperate to revive the good moment, rushed forward and seized her hand, saying, "Look, honey," as Steve parted the membrane to reveal the steamy organs, "look, honey, it's got kidneys and heart and liver and everything, just like you and me."

My wife is a strong woman who has cleaned wormy fish with me and can rip the breast out of a grouse with one hand. But for some reason what I said about the sheep organs failed to revive her enthusiasm. I glared at Steve, muttering my thanks to him, and after noticing the sheep's head lying open-eyed in the dirt with its dead tongue licking some old birch leaves, I drew my foot back and kicked that head like a soccer ball.

That was no soccer ball. It rolled lopsidedly away and sent me straight into the air, clutching my boot and howling.

"Get that head," Steve warned, "or it'll bring dogs."

So I retrieved the head (which had not gone far at all, if you have ever tried to kick a cinder block), glad that my kick had at least amused my wife, if only at my expense. Plainly, though, she was no longer happily immersed in the beautiful hungry scheme of things, and it vexed me that Steve and Ernie began to poke fun at the woman now that she was down, Steve inventorying the organs with a flourish and Ernie yum-yumming at the good edible ones while dropping the more dubious organs into a plastic trash bag.

We lowered the carcass from the crossbar and returned to the corral for a second lamb.

Let me say one thing. There is often a code among men about what may properly be said and not, and sometimes I find this code regrettable, and even unpatriotic, if it hinders free speech. For example, I could not bring myself to alert Ernie to the splash of sheep's blood on his hearing aid, it would have been presumptuous and nitpicking of me. Likewise, as the greenhorn in the group, I was unwilling to suggest to Steve and Ernie that in preparation for the second lamb we should take the time to sharpen our knives. And I will forever marvel—for later we discussed the matter—that three men can be thinking the same thing at the same moment and not one of them be willing to speak it.

Simon the ram charged us as we approached, and as usual he came up short, gasping at the end of his rope. Steve walked up to him with an empty bucket and presented himself as a tall and gangly target to Simon, standing sideways like a Spanish matador, and when Simon charged, Steve swung the bucket down and zonked him on the head with it. Poor Simon lolled and probably saw stars. This was the sort of thing Steve had done with himself since Becky ran off. He said he was trying to cure Simon of bad habits.

Meanwhile Merry squatted by the corral fence, talking softly to the ewe named Daphne and reaching in to pet her. And as I watched them, the black-haired, creamy-skinned woman and the black-faced, creamy-fleeced ewe, the sun having brightened above us and the air grown as warm as forty degrees, I had a feeling of wild chamomile tea seeping downward through my innards and settling around my loins. It was a good feeling, of strength and life, and yet I couldn't help noticing at the edges of the pasture the rusty fireweed stalks that foretold winter, and I couldn't help thinking of the end that Steve and Becky had come to, and it seemed to me a shame that change vies so unremittingly with our happiness. I gazed at my wife, wanting more than ever to take her on a lovers' walk through the woods this evening, and I knew we men had better do a neat job of this next lamb if we were not to jeopardize my walk.

The marked lamb came along sweetly enough, a very lamby lamb he was, following Ernie and Steve and Merry and me as its new herd. But as soon as we arrived at the place of the red flag—and it may have been the red flag itself that spooked the lamb, or the assortment of knives on the sheet of plywood, or the spruce shadows at play, or the camp robbers nipping at the sheepskin that we had draped over a sawhorse, or maybe just the smell of the blood of its predecessor— but that lamby lamb stopped prancing and turned and galloped all the way back to the corral.

We followed, and Steve caught the lamb and haltered it. The lamb refused to budge, so Steve yanked on the halter, and when the lamb dug in, he naturally lashed at it with the halter shank. Ernie chuckled at these doings, but me, I stomped my foot, I cried, "Steve, that is no way to treat an animal!" Which was unusually silly of me to say, since only yesterday Steve had seen me deliver a frank blow to our neighbor's ill-mannered hound with a broomstick. But Steve is my friend, never more so than at that moment when I chided him for beating the lamb. He didn't call me hypocrite or gape incredulously, but only glanced at Merry and seemed to recognize that I was in the transcendental presence of my love.

We men carried our lamby lamb back to the place of the red flag, plumped it down on the plywood, and conferred in whispers. I was vehement that we should cut this lamb and not shoot it, I wouldn't have us string up a second lamb only to see it open its eyes and look around at the world. Steve and Ernie agreed, so Ernie, who has a casual way of doing just about everything he does, picked up a knife, drew it once, twice across his pantleg, then squatted beside the lamb and ever so casually pushed the blade in under its ear. The lamb bucked and squirmed, and I anxiously fell on it like a football player on a football. Ernie grunted, withdrew the knife, peeked under the lamb's chin, then reinserted the knife and gradually sawed across the width of its throat while the lamb, open-eyed, stared straight ahead.

As this operation continued into its second minute, I heard sighs of dismay coming from Merry. Ernie was making slow progress, his knife catching in the lamb's thick wool, and yet he was humming to himself, which annoyed me extremely. I stared at Ernie's hearing aid and gritted through my teeth that perhaps he would like to try a sharper knife. "Huh?" He withdrew the knife and raised his bloody fingers by his face as though he were lifting welding goggles. "What'd ya say?" Merry stepped closer and stared down at us, and

I smiled up at her, relaxing my grip on the lamb so as not to appear foolish. It was at this point that the lamb took off.

That lamb took off and towed me over the plywood, knocked Steve down and left us in a four-legged muddle. "Drug you through the dirt," Steve yelled. "Get that lamb!" We jumped after it, and I heard Ernie chuckling behind us as we pursued the poor creature, its loosened head rising and falling as it bounded back to the corral.

It was a hushed and sobering scene that we found there. Daphne the ewe and all the other lambs stood gathered at the fence looking out at our lamby lamb, and our lamby lamb stood looking in. Its forelegs were spaced widely in the grass, the better to hold itself up. Blood was swaying from the torn flaps of its throat, and steam rose from the blood. The lamb was having trouble breathing and there seemed to be a great weight on its head, which it held low. Steve and Ernie and I kept our distance, as this lamb was not going to run anywhere ever again. Merry, when I looked at her, was standing apart from us, eyeing us as though we were strangers to her.

"What a mess," she said.

"What in blazes does a two-months-pregnant woman want with watching a sheep slaughter anyhow," I yelled.

"You've really made a mess of it." Her body heaved up as if she were in pain, pulling up at the shoulders and sinking with a sigh.

"Is that all you can say? We botched it?"

"You don't understand anything."

"What don't I understand?"

"You see? That's exactly what I mean."

"No, I don't see. What are you talking about?" I watched her heading back to the house, all sorts of nasty thoughts running through my head. "So we botched it," I yelled. "You're not so smart. Maybe you don't understand either."

Or maybe we understood each other only too well.

I averted my face to hide my consternation from my friends. And as I watched Simon the ram charging the air and pulling at his rope, pulling his stake askew in the pasture, I couldn't picture myself closing on our lamby lamb with a knife in my hand. I asked Steve and Ernie if they wouldn't mind dispatching the other sheep without me, and tomorrow I would help them to clean the skins, because right now I had somewhere to go. Fool that I am, all I could think about was saving our promised lovers' walk through the woods.

The Ballad of Robbie Fox

I ndians call me white boy, white people call me salmon cruncher. My skin's white and I'm pretty hairy but I'll never be white. The village Indians used to chase me around and call me white boy, that's why I moved to Fairbanks. The older I get I mostly hang out with halfbreeds.

People don't like you if you're too different from them, but like Chief Walter Northway says in his autobiography, people got to intermix, all the clans get stronger then. Like I had this dog Skookum once, part Lab and part husky, a little bit of everything, and tough, too, he got quilled in the face by a porcupine, got hit in the ass with birdshot, but he was tough as nails, and good-mannered, too, I mean, sleeping in my tent he'd curl up at my feet and not wake me till morning then crawl up and lick my face like—time to get up, Robbie!

It's like living in two worlds, man. I got this uncle who's a total bush rat, lives out on the river past Eagle, trapping and cutting wood and—real traditional life, you know? Soon as I come back from dive school in San Diego, I go out in the bush and live with him and fish with him and it's weird cause they got all those malls in San Diego and tons of people and cars and you come back and it's so different, quiet and peaceful with trees all around.

I was smoking a joint once with a Jewish guy on my fire crew and there were two Indians pretending they were digging lice from each other's hair going *What, you think I'm Jewish or something?* all giggling pretending they're in a concentration camp talking about this war movie they saw and they don't even know he's a Jewish guy sitting there smoking a joint with me all wooden like one of them tobacco store Indians. It's all bullshit, man. Different clothes people wear, that's all. It's all games and nothing changes.

You still got to do something, though. I had a good job as a cook on a oil rig down in Louisiana till I got busted DWI in New Orleans and there was this black dude in jail I played cards and smoked cigarettes with who cracked me up all the time like "I was in Angola for three years and I didn't jerk off one time, man," he's all proud, "but one night I dreamed I was getting some hootchie and guess what? When I woke up in the morning I was fucking my bed! What was I thinking!" I don't want to go to no heavy-ass prison like that, man, steal livers from the prison kitchen and jerk off with them back in their cells. Big guy comes up to the little guy and says, "It's time," and the little guy's all, "No, please don't, I got AIDS," and the big guy, "That's all right, little man, so do I."

If only I didn't have a record, Special Forces would've taken me. I was thinking about joining the

French Foreign Legion. I'd do it for nothing, man, I just want the training, be able to do the cool stuff, rappelling down the cliffs and all. We should go to school and meet people and make something better of ourselves. Seattle, Los Angeles, Disneyland, Mexico, rub shoulders with people, you know what I'm saying? When I was in Fairbanks Correctional I was reading law books trying to figure out how my life could work for me if I could get a loan or something, start with a piece of land, have my own place instead of scrounging all the time—buy property, sell it, buy a little more, see, that's how you move up in the world. I'm gonna wear a big old fucking gold ring on my finger like Tony Montana. Yeah, hook up with someone in Mexico, someone with kilos, you know, the big shit, not messing around with peewees all the time, I mean, if you're gonna do something you might as well do it. These dudes I knew in jail, they all got after-hours joints with slot machines and growing operations, big old wads of cash they walk into Cheap Charlie's with, gold watches, gold rings, they even got legitimate businesses, auto detailing and stuff. That's how I want us to be, enough money so we can take off sometime, have margaritas on the beach. I don't want to be stuck in Fairbanks, Alaska. I want to jump in a convertible GT and go driving down the road, hop on a plane to paradise, man, I'm saying, dudes, trust me, I've been there, I've been all over. When I was gonna learn underwater welding in California, I was standing barefoot on the beach and the breeze was blowing my hair and the sand was rubbing my toes and some fine-ass blonde chick walks by…Nothing like that ever happens here, man, this state is for peasants, we're worker-ant motherfuckers, we're a labor pool, we never get to get out and enjoy things.

When I was thirteen I was dead four days comatose from thirteen hits of triple-dip gold king. In my head it was holy wars: good and evil. There was this pinhole of light ahead of me and these voices around me going *Robbie, Robbie Fox, come over on this side, man—No, no, Robbie, over here, man, over here* and the light got bigger and bigger ahead of me and I finally woke up again all soft and warm in a fetal position like I was born out of a woman's pussy.

I've been in and out of homes since I was thirteen, see, I'm tired. There's a couple of things I'm thinking about doing. Being a smokejumper: that'd be cool. This girl I used to date, I saw her down at the Big Lake fire, she won't even look at me now, she got on a Hotshot crew and is going to college and everything, really got her shit together I guess. You know what's a good thing to do is asbestos cleanup. Get thirty bucks an hour off the bat and there's a high demand for it, that's what my cousin Herbie says, once you get your license you've got it made and no one can take it away from you, piss test or no piss test.

I was a father when I was fifteen, my daughter's eight years old now. My aunt says I'm like a middle-aged man I've been through so much. I want my own place, I want to settle down. And I firmly believe that if you do what's right, the rest will take care of itself. Like when I was in dive school in California, my grandma sent me money so I could have my daughter with me, and it was just like I had dreamed it would be when I was alone all strung out on the beach crying because I wished I had my daughter with me. Dreams come true, dudes. But when you're doing the wrong thing, I'm telling you, it finds you out, it catches up to you. Dr. Death, he's gonna scope you out. Like I was dealing coke for two years, just the powder, people who do the hard shit are too snaky for me, and I was hurting people, good people, and I knew it, too, selling joints for ten bucks a pinner in firecamp is one thing, but the coke thing started getting to me, I felt this shadow around me, chilling me, and that was Dr. Death, you know what I'm saying? There was this dancer I knew, Jeanette, a really beautiful girl, but she comes over one day wanting to score some coke and I stood back and really looked at her and—she was fucked up, man, all shivery and *ggghhaaaaa* and hollow-eyed and I told her to leave, man, just get out of here, I'm not selling this shit to you no more. Dr. Death!

I'll tell you what happened to me that night. I was whacked all day, all shaking and seeing that shadow around me. I was *afraid,* man. Afraid I'd never light up good anymore. Afraid of nothing, afraid of everything, afraid how everything looks like nothing and nothing is all there is. And I got in my car and went driving that night. Yeah, I was driving through this neighborhood with a knife in my hand *afraid* and I was riding the steering wheel looking out the window at people's houses *afraid* looking left and right at people's houses *afraid afraid* and it was a dark night and my heart was beating so bad it hurt *afraid afraid* and I had the knife in my hand and this shadow was swallowing me up *afraid afraid afraid* and I wanted to kill somebody, man, I mean anybody, I couldn't stop myself, and if any little thing happened, if a lady came out of her house and hooked her dog on its chain, I was gonna do it, man, I'm sweating and trembling and my heart's on fire *afraid afraid afraid afraid* and I looked at the knife in my hand and I'm all *What the hell! What the hell are you doing, Robbie!*

And that's when I threw the knife on the floor and I drove over to this church I know and parked there till morning kind of talking myself down and praying and I was so totally wiped out I even cried.

Like it says in the Bible, see, God gave man to have a reprobate mind. You're born to know right and wrong. People kill and steal and are totally wicked, but if you keep doing the wrong thing, pretty soon you won't know the difference anymore, and that's when the nightmare starts. You might think it's weird, but I remember these big fucking hard-ass dudes in jail all singing high to Jesus and clapping hands and thanking him for stopping them selling drugs and hurting people and they were glad they got caught. Yes, glad. But it's not easy. Every time you try to go clean, someone drops a big bag of coke on your table and—I got this shit, man, take half, go sell it and pay me later. Or just when you tell yourself you're gonna stop chasing pussy and go forward instead of sideways for a change, some chick calls you on the phone and she's all *Oh Robbie Robbie Fox I haven't seen you in so long* and you're *Okay baby come on over but just this once* and thank God God's so busy because you got an appointment with him sooner or later and no can hide, man, all hangdog looking at yourself in the mirror going What happened, Robbie, what happened to your fine promises? And next time you swear it's going to be different, next time she calls on the telephone you're standing there with wings and a big sword trying to cut the phone line saying *So long, baby* you're hanging tough *So long cause this is the new Robbie you're talking to, the new and improved Robbie, the new improved and reincarnated Robbie Fox!* Yeah!

Fishes and Wine

Jimmy Biggs had journeyed to Alaska all the way from Tucson hoping to make enough money to pay for college one day. Whenever an older hand like Ratface, tramping the beach beside him, asked Jimmy how he liked cannery work, Jimmy answered that he didn't mind it for now but he wanted to do something better with his life. He was nineteen.

Ahead of them, Lucky Tyler marched over the wet sand with a strut, swinging his arms as if to keep time with some inner passion. When he stopped to wait for them, he hooked his thumbs in his beltloops and hiked up his jeans and shouted "Let's go, turkeys!" Tyler was a squat man with a large head and a thick nose that doglegged from an old break. A Pancho Villa mustache swooped down the sides of his mouth.

"What's his hurry?" Ratface grumbled.

"You didn't hear about the bet?" Jimmy said.

A party had started up in the bunkhouse shortly after dinner, and as soon as it was obvious that there wouldn't be enough booze to keep everybody happy, these three had agreed to make the run into Naknek, the only town in walking distance on this remote shore of Bristol Bay. The cannery's two forklift drivers— Lucky Tyler was one of them—always vied for popularity among the lesser line workers, and when the second forklift driver heard that Lucky Tyler was going to town, he laughed scornfully and gave odds that Tyler wouldn't make it back to the cannery before midnight.

"Hell if I care about his bet," Ratface said. "I'm on my own time."

"That goes double for me," Jimmy said, glad to have nobody to answer to for a change. It was late in May, the herring run had ended, and for the first time in weeks he had an evening off.

The end of a bandage dangled from under Jimmy's blue flannel cuff, and as he walked he tried stuffing the bandage back around his wrist. His wrist ached from tendonitis contracted from handling too many herring too diligently—scooping the fish off conveyor belts, packing them into waxed boxes for export—and whenever his wrist ached especially much he told himself, This is all part of doing something with your life, Jimmy boy, eight-hour days'll be a cinch after this.

The three men walked abreast, picking their way among the slick dark rocks. Muddy bluffs rose to their left, buttressing the tundra, and to their right a shining mudflat sloped a hundred or more yards to the water. The tide was out, and far out there you could see the fish tenders lying at anchor. A few lights glimmered on the boats but it was early yet, not half past eight, barely twilight in this part of Alaska.

"What's your hurry," Ratface demanded.

Lucky Tyler had gotten ahead again. "I'm thirsty, that's what."

"No, it's that other forklift driver," Ratface said.

"That old motherfucker said I can't hike three miles twice and bring back a rack of beer without falling on my ass."

Jimmy drew closer. "He only said that to get you to go out and buy the beer."

"Damn right," Tyler said.

Ratface was doubled over in one of his coughing fits, scarlet-faced, his mouth wide open.

"Quit coughing on us," Tyler said.

"Can't you cover your mouth?" Jimmy said.

"Goddammit I told you it ain't contagious," Ratface cried, and lashed his empty duffel bag, the one they had brought to carry the booze in, against a rock.

Ratface was a slight and beady-eyed man who had been drifting on the seafood circuit for years. He always ate his meals alone and as soon as he was done eating he would get up and leave the mess hall. Many years ago Ratface had gone to Cuba to pick sugar cane for Fidel Castro and nobody knew what to make of him when he told them this. He was often seen talking to himself.

"You should've seen it when that old motherfucker dropped his pallet," Lucky Tyler was still stewing about his nemesis back at the bunkhouse. "Drove his forklift smack into the freezer door and dropped two thousand pounds of fish. Cary Sue saw it."

"Cary Sue," Ratface muttered balefully.

"Crashed his forklift and he's got the nerve to tell me he's a better driver."

"He said he's better than you?" Jimmy said.

"Calls me a forklift *driver*," Tyler said. "He's a forklift *operator* but I'm a forklift *driver*."

"That's just words," Jimmy said.

"You like Cary Sue?" Ratface asked.

"Sure, I like her," Jimmy said.

"You don't care if she's a dyke?"

"No, I don't care," Jimmy said.

"Well," Ratface said after a moment, "neither do I. But I wish she was more up front with us about it."

"Maybe she didn't think we'd follow her orders if she told us on the first day she's a dyke," Jimmy said.

"It spoils everything when the foreman's not up front with you," Ratface said.

"Hell, I like her," Tyler said. "It's a shame, though."

"What about?" Ratface said.

"It's a shame when a woman's getting more pussy than I do, but she's a damn good foreman," Lucky Tyler explained.

The others laughed. Lucky Tyler lit a cigarette. He was called Lucky Tyler because a bomb burst his foxhole in Vietnam twenty years ago and he was the only man of three to come up out of it. He wore a brown corduroy jacket over his t-shirt, the dirty white t-shirt bulging over his belly.

A cold wind was whisking around them and Jimmy buttoned the top buttons of his flannel. They still had a half mile to go up the beach and another mile inland into town. They walked briskly, sometimes tossing stones along the shore or pivoting and hurling them at the black face of the bluff. Up there on the bluff a line of old cabins straggled, abandoned until June when the setnetters would return to fish for salmon.

"That old motherfucker only gave me six bucks for drinks," Tyler said.

"Quit thinking about him," Jimmy said.

"I can't help it. How much cash'd you guys draw from your checks?"

"I took fifteen," Jimmy said.

"Twenty," Ratface said.

"Now why do you suppose that old bastard motherfucker only gave me six bucks?"

"Maybe that's all the money he had," Jimmy said.

Lucky Tyler threw down his cigarette and hitched up his jeans the way he always did before mounting his forklift. "Let me see my paycheck, Jimmy."

"I don't have it."

"You don't have it?"

"I left it under the bunk."

"You did not."

"The idea was you weren't gonna cash your check," Jimmy said. "What's it matter if I don't have it if you're not gonna cash it?"

"I'm not gonna cash it, I just wanna see it." Lucky Tyler stopped walking and frowned at him, and Jimmy pulled uneasily at the bandage trailing from his wrist. He withdrew some checks from his back pocket and handed one to Tyler.

"Hah, you see!"

"The kid was doing you a favor," Ratface said.

"Then why's he tell me he hasn't got my check when he's got it right there in his back pocket?"

"I don't care," Jimmy walked ahead, "I really don't care about your check."

"Hey, I'm sorry," Tyler called after him.

When they caught up to Jimmy, Lucky Tyler asked him again to guard his paycheck.

"No way. It's your check, you do what you want with it. Just don't ask me to cash mine."

"I won't."

"I'm not touching mine till I put it in the bank."

"Fine."

"All right then." Jimmy plucked the check from Tyler's hand and slipped it in his back pocket. Then they turned and watched Ratface, who had gone over by a driftwood log and was bent over hawking, shooting phlegm from his mouth.

"That sounds bad," Tyler said.

"You all right?" Jimmy said.

Ratface nodded and they walked on.

"How can you be sure it's not contagious?" Tyler said.

"Because it's cured," Ratface said wiping his mouth.

"I didn't know they could cure TB."

"Well now you know," Ratface said. "Almost had my lung cut out."

Lucky Tyler threw his hands up and said to Jimmy, "You see why a guy wants a drink now and then?"

"I know why a guy wants a drink," Jimmy said, "but I don't know why anyone would work for three weeks and blow his paycheck in three hours."

"No one's blowing any check," Tyler said. "I just hope a hundred cash'll cover what we need."

"It should be plenty," Jimmy said.

"That old motherfucker only gave me six bucks," Tyler said. "I know what things cost. It's seven bucks for a sixpack of Rainier."

"That's the cheapest they got?" Jimmy said.

"Cheapest brand. Twenty-two dollars a case. Hell, I don't wanna drink with that old fart anyway."

"I'd like to pour some Calvert down Cary Sue's throat and see what happens to her," Ratface said.

"Like what might happen to her?" Jimmy said.

"I don't know. But it ruins everything when the foreman's not up front with you."

To their left some water was flowing down a gully that slanted down the face of the bluff to the beach. They danced their way up this gully to the top and then jogged across the tundra looking for the dirt road that Tyler and Ratface said was nearby, jumping from tussock to tussock to avoid the water in the low places. It was still early in the year, May, and the grass was not very green yet, just a flat expanse of dull grasses and mosses and low berry plants stretching for miles.

Once they had found the dirt road, they slowed again to a walk. In the distance Jimmy saw a radio tower poking up from the flatness.

"I was working in a pea cannery down in Walla Walla," Lucky Tyler reflected. "There's a little college down there with a heated duck pond, can you believe it? I used to ride by on my bicycle."

Jimmy had rolled his sleeve back from his wrist and was trying to reattach the clip on his loose bandage. "How do you know it was heated?"

"I'm telling you, it was heated," Lucky Tyler said. "To keep the ice off it. So the college kids could have ducks to watch."

"College kids," Ratface said. "That explains it."

"Man, was I sick of peas," Tyler said. "We'd go out behind the cannery and pee in the pea field just to do it. Someone's peas might have my pee in it, ha!"

"I worked on a surimi ship where we did the same thing," Ratface said. "Just peed right there in the fish."

"I'll never eat another green pea as long as I live," Tyler said. "I couldn't even eat dinner tonight."

"You don't like stew?" Jimmy said.

"I love beef stew but not if there's peas in it."

"Get yourself something in town," Ratface said.

"Yeah, maybe I'll get a cheeseburger," Tyler said.

"Should be enough time for it and still make it back before midnight," Jimmy said.

It was late twilight, nine o'clock or so. Pink and violet undershimmers swam in the evening sky and reminded Jimmy, not happily, of a school of herring. The road to town was rutted from whatever few trucks had driven here and back; there really was nowhere to drive but on the dirt roads that petered out across the tundra. To their right the treeless sweep was interrupted by a silvery little pond.

"How much'd you bet him you'd be back before midnight?" Ratface asked.

"Thirty-five bucks," Tyler said.

"That's why he only gave you six," Jimmy said. "He knew he'd lose the bet."

Tyler nodded sourly. "Maybe I'll spend his six on my cheeseburger and not give him any beer."

"Oh, I don't know," Jimmy said.

"Don't know what?" Tyler said.

"If that'd be fair."

Tyler ignored that and lit a cigarette. "Maybe I'm a little out of shape," he said, "but he's dead wrong if he thinks I'm a soft gut." He blew his cigarette smoke at Ratface.

"Cut it out," Ratface said.

Lucky Tyler elbowed Jimmy. "I didn't think people even *got* tuberculosis anymore, did you, Jimmy?"

"I don't *have* tuberculosis," Ratface said. "That was ten years ago."

"When I got out of jump school I had a twenty-eight waist," Tyler said. "Asshole tells me I got a soft gut."

Jimmy unwound the flapping bandage from his wrist and stuffed it in his pocket.

"I'm short one toe and got rebar in my leg and my hearing's fucked up and some old queen tells me I got a soft gut?" Tyler had quickened his pace and Jimmy and Ratface hopped to keep up with him.

"It just don't matter what he told you," Ratface said.

Tyler grunted and glanced at Jimmy. "You hear me, Tucson?"

"I don't think you're fat," Jimmy said.

Tyler grabbed a roll of flesh at his side and with his fist began beating himself in the belly. While he walked he kept slugging himself as if he were beating a drum.

"I'm Airborne," he yelled, "I'm an Airborne mother-fucker and don't anybody forget it!"

"Why don't we get a drink before starting back," Ratface said. "We'll stop in at Fisher's."

"Maybe so," Tyler said hotly.

"Fisher's a bar?" Jimmy asked.

"That's right," Tyler said. And to Ratface, "Help me figure this out. If we get four cases of beer, that's eighty-eight bucks. Plus a bottle of tequila would throw us over a hundred. You remember how much Nat gave me?"

"No."

"There probably won't be time to stop in any bar," Jimmy said.

"But I know Bandy gave you his whole draw," Ratface said.

"Then he gets his fair share," Tyler said. "Fair is fair. But if a guy gives me six bucks—I'll tell you one thing, the only bottle I spring for that old lard-ass fork-lift operator is the one he splits his lip on."

"There might not be time to get a cheeseburger if we start going in the bars," Jimmy said.

Lucky Tyler looked at him. "Listen, Tucson, the only way we can fill this duffel bag is if we go in a bar. The liquor store is part of the bar. They sell from stock in the back room. That's how it is in this town."

"He's right," Ratface said.

"You don't have to drink a drop," Tyler said. "Course they won't cash your check for you unless you buy a drink with it."

"Nobody's cashing any checks," Jimmy said.

"I'm just telling you how it works," Tyler said.

"That's how it works, is it?" Jimmy slowed his pace but the others pulled him along. "The whole economy's just fishes and wine. You make your money and give it right back to them. Of course they're happy to cash your check as long as they get a piece of it."

"No," Tyler said, "the only reason we'll need to cash a check is if that bottle of tequila throws us over a hundred."

"It's one bar or another," Ratface said.

Jimmy gazed ahead at the dusky faceless buildings of the town. He saw nobody on the outskirts. "What's the choice?"

"Well, there's one bar not even worthy mentioning," Lucky Tyler said. "And the Red Dog has some chairs and tables in it. That's a nice place for a college kid to sit. And then there's Fisher's."

"Fisher's," Jimmy said. "We'll go there."

Ratface let out a strange yip when he heard they were going to Fisher's.

Lucky Tyler said, "Now listen, Jimmy, don't tick anyone off in there, all right?"

Naknek is built on the bank of a river, and coming into town they saw the water edging silently by, broad and smooth and faintly aglow. Warehouses and canneries fronted the river and yardlights shone down from the high roof corners. Seagulls stood below in the circles of light.

They passed a grocery store and a hardware store, both shut for the night. Ratface and Lucky Tyler crossed the road to a sunken wooden building with a light burning on the porch. Jimmy heard men's voices inside. A white mutt got up on the porch and wagged its tail at them. Ratface and Lucky Tyler tramped noisily up the porch steps and Jimmy followed more grimly. The saloon doors swung inward when they entered and swung shut behind them.

Heads turned and Jimmy swiped the cap off his head. The bar ran around three sides of the room and men stood along the length of it. Pool balls clacked in the heart of the room where men shot pool under low-hanging lamps. It was crowded inside with just enough elbow room but no empty stools to be had. The place was smoky and full of talk. Jimmy kept his eyes moving or he met with unfriendly stares. They were wiry men, their faces creased and bearded and stained.

Lucky Tyler and Ratface gravitated toward the white-aproned bartender, and Jimmy went after them. "We buy the stuff and go," he whispered.

Tyler nodded, but distractedly, bargazing at all the colored bottles and pretty glasses. With his thumb and forefinger he kept smoothing down the sides of his mustache. He raised his hand to catch the bartender's attention.

The only woman in the joint was high up in the corner on a video screen, a young blonde wriggling around on a tropical beach. Jimmy watched her doing what she was doing for a minute until he realized nobody else was watching. When the bartender approached, Jimmy turned his back and tried to concentrate on the game of pool. "You know how to play snooker?" Ratface asked him.

"No." Jimmy felt warm and undid a shirt button.

Lucky Tyler finally rejoined them and said he had placed the order.

"Good. Ten o'clock," Jimmy said. "We'll make it."

"Where's the booze?" Ratface asked.

"Bartender's packing the duffel bag," Tyler said. He watched the game with them a minute, then cautiously cleared his throat and hiked up his jeans. "Can I see my check, Jimmy?"

Jimmy stared at the green of the pool table. "What for?"

"I just wanna see it."

"We brought enough cash to cover things."

Lucky Tyler wiped his hands on his hips. "Well maybe I want something for myself."

Jimmy looked at him and looked away again.

"Tucson, man, I already ordered us a round. Ten bucks is all."

Jimmy turned and saw the bartender setting down three Budweisers: brown bottles, bright red and blue on the labels. Some stools had come available and the bartender murmured *Sit down, boys* and Tyler went ahead and sat down. Jimmy turned to Ratface but Ratface only shook his head and said, "Hey, I'm a drinking man too, but if a guy is dumb enough to blow his paycheck on booze, I'm not gonna stop him."

Jimmy took the third stool. A thin, unshaven man slouched next to him, head propped on his hand and grinning bleary-eyed at Jimmy. The man's lips were shut and moving in a circle as if he were chewing tobacco. Goddamn, he stank. Like the bottom of a herring hold he stank. Jimmy turned away but the stranger clamped a hand on his shoulder and hissed words in his ear. Jimmy shoved the hand away and sat rigid, his heart bucking. He didn't know what the man had said and he didn't ask.

Lucky Tyler demanded his paycheck again and this time Jimmy gave it to him. Tyler unfolded it, and there was just that piece of paper he had sweated for, pale and fragile in his palm.

A hush had come over the room. The men around the bar had stopped talking and they all seemed to glance at Lucky Tyler as if they had a stake in his paycheck, as if they had seen this little drama many times before. Their keen, sad faces made Jimmy shiver.

Jimmy looked up again at the girl on the video screen, but nobody in the bar gave a damn about her and neither at the moment did Jimmy. In Lucky Tyler he was looking down through the insides of a man to a region where all duties and scruples blow along like dry leaves before a fire. There is no answer for that— none Jimmy could give, and none he wanted to give, as he found even a kid named Jimmy Biggs could be so indifferent from the height of a barstool.

Lucky Tyler handed his paycheck to the bartender and received cash in return, and Jimmy heard what sounded like a long sigh go up through the room, followed by a riffle of long swallows and a soft knocking of glasses one by one upon the bar.

One Less Black Bear

By morning they all knew a black bear had come into base camp. When Leon heard about it he went and looked at the pit where they had stored their fresh food and saw just a couple of steaks left in the bottom and a hunk of yellow cheese. He had lain in his tent last night listening to the chopped roar of a helicopter and the drone of an engine taking water from the pond and meanwhile the bear had torn the Visqueen cover from the pit and taken the steaks and hot dogs and gone off into the woods leaving behind some plastic wrappers and a pile of scat. After a successful raid like that there was little question the bear would be back.

It was a warm, muggy morning, the daylight yellowy brown from all the smoke. At Supply, Leon sprayed himself over with mosquito dope and got some water boiling on a Coleman stove. John Ritchie, who had been on duty since midnight, leaned against some boxes by the supply tent, smoking a cigarette and staring red-eyed at Leon.

John Ritchie looked scooped out by a spoon, he was that thin and sunken. He had the word *John* tattooed in blue on his inside right forearm. He was a quarter Athabaskan like Leon himself and boasted of the checks he would soon get from a new program Uncle Sam was running with one of the Native corporations. In these seasonal jobs you knew about another man only what he told you. In Leon's case you couldn't tell by looking at him that any part of him was Indian, and since it had never mattered much to Leon anyway, he seldom talked about it.

For his breakfast he boiled an MRE packet of meatballs in tomato sauce and he offered John Ritchie some coffee. "Busy night?"

"Nah." Ritchie sat down. "Couple crews came in from spike camp."

"Any word on the fire?"

"They're talking about trying a backfire." His eyes closed over the smoke from his cigarette. "You heard about the blackie?"

"Yeah." The meatballs tasted good and Leon didn't miss the steak he might be eating if it hadn't been for the black bear. The fresh food was sent into the field every few days but after a while the fresh food thing grew old and it seemed easier just to tear open another MRE.

"They're gonna shoot it," John Ritchie said.

"I figured."

"These jokers in overhead." Ritchie laughed his gimpy weak-chested laugh. "Can't kill a bear without going up the chain of command."

"They call it in to Fairbanks?"

"Yeah, they're calling in a ranger and a shotgun."

Leon nodded and drank his coffee. It was a shame about the black bear but he wasn't surprised. What would surprise him was if the bear didn't come back for another meal or if the ranger didn't shoot it. The trouble was that nothing had surprised Leon Clayton in a long, a very long time.

Thirty yards away, the camp crew from Tolmin were building a new wall tent for the medic. Nelson, the youngest on the crew, was cutting spruce poles with a chainsaw while the others held the poles for him. Silver smoke was blowing from the chainsaw and Nelson finally killed the engine and headed toward Supply. He came bare-chested, his hair long and black, a red bandanna at his forehead. He smiled uneasily at Leon and glanced at John Ritchie. Leon wished the boy wouldn't feel uneasy with them and asked him what he needed. The boy said he needed oil for his chainsaw.

John Ritchie coiled up on his box. "We saw your chainsaw smoking, Nelson. Wondered if you'd ever figure it out."

"We figured it out." Nelson's brown body tautened as he reached back to scratch a mosquito bite.

Leon gave him a quart of bar-and-chain oil for the chainsaw. "What happened to the medic's tent?"

"It blew down," Nelson said.

"Didn't build it right the first time?" Ritchie said.

"We didn't build it the first time," Nelson said.

Leon laughed at this, at John Ritchie's expense. The boy knelt with his chainsaw, unscrewed the cap from the oil reservoir and filled it with oil. The muscles flexed across his chest and his smooth brown arms worked easily over the saw. After he was done, he returned to his crew, and Leon watched them, three of them fitting a ridgepole into the sleeve at the top of the medic's tent, the others lashing together a tripod of spruce poles. There was Charley the elder and crew boss, and young Nelson who did the work of two men, Larry who grumbled about the white man every chance he got, Cathy and Mary who giggled all the time and made eyes at Leon, fat Floyd who played country guitar at a bar in Fairbanks, and Benjamin the artist who painted all the signs around firecamp using orange paint on plywood, Athabaskans all of them, mostly full-blooded, and it was rare Leon ever wondered what it might be like to be like Nelson, full-blooded and living in a village with others like himself, but it happened sometimes.

He had eaten with them last night, and when they laughed about the white man thinking he could put out the fire, he had laughed too, because it was indeed a strange business, fighting fire, the way the white man dragged fax machines into the woods, the way he started small fires to foil the big fire, the way the Incident Commander chewed Rolaids all day while scanning the ridgetops with his binoculars.

But the laughter had a bleaker side, as Leon saw it, because the white man was paying the camp crew from Tolmin to do something they found ridiculous. Deep Pockets fought the fire each summer and the Natives all over Alaska helped him to do it. You couldn't blame anybody, but Leon felt he couldn't live with the contradictions so many of them lived with, or calculate the fractions of his bloodline in terms of the coin it would bring him, and so he kept to himself. He plowed snow in Fairbanks in the winter and he worked on fires like this one in the summer and he went it alone. You've got to live your own life, he thought. Others will try to get you to live theirs: don't do it. Always trying to have a piece of you, make you an ally or an enemy, the Cowboys and the Indians—what had all the spear chuckers and whiskey traders in the world to do with him? I'm me. Man. Leon. Free. Me, Leon Clayton, and he often felt the real person in him was a wild free animal others wanted to pen and that made him bitter and aloof.

The fire was burning over the ridge in the next valley. There was no individual smoke column, only a diffuse, dusty haze. Toward noon the sun passed higher in the sky and shone as a thin red disk. At Supply, Leon took inventory and called in orders on the radio. John Ritchie knew some drivers in Ground Support, buddies from the Laborers Union, and he spent time with them or else he slouched among the boxes at Supply, complaining to Leon about the supervisor and about the long hours.

"Get some sleep," Leon told him. "I'll cover things."

After lunch the ranger drove into camp in a green pickup truck. A squat man with a bushy mustache climbed out of the truck in a tan uniform and stiffened in the muggy heat. The ic and a delegation from Logistics came and peered into the ranger's gun case, and they led him into the woods and showed him the food pit which the black bear had plundered. Later

Leon saw him sitting in his truck with his windows rolled up against the mosquitos, waiting for nightfall.

The afternoon went quietly. The supervisor gave Leon an hour off to take a bath. They were thirty miles south of the Yukon River, base camp set between a pond and a creek in the middle of thousands of acres of tinder-dry spruce. This was bear country. Around two o'clock Leon was running through the woods along the creek, looking for the sandbar where he liked to kneel and wash his hair, when he heard a crunch of branches nearby and he stopped. The bear for sure, he thought.

He heard a repeated crunch of branches and then some grunts and a rhythmic thrashing as if the bear were scraping up a root or wrestling with an old log. A moment later he understood his mistake when he heard a soft exchange of men's voices and a laugh. The laugh had a familiar gimpy sound, as if it had come out of one lung, and Leon, shifting his head, was able to make out John Ritchie's profile, gleaming with sweat or was it insect repellent, his naked chest and shoulders pitifully limp and pale among the branches.

It was an odd place to go unclothed. Leon smelled marijuana, pungent like burning spruce. Ritchie was smoking with somebody, one of his union sidekicks maybe, and as Leon continued along the creek, swatting the mosquitos with his cap, he was angry that Ritchie always complained about getting no sleep when here he was fooling around and getting stoned.

After bathing Leon returned to camp. John Ritchie showed up later and they listened on the radio to news of blowups along the fireline. At three o'clock

Communications relayed to Supply an order for drip torches and bladder bags and they loaded these items into the brown Ford. John Ritchie panted and worked in spurts.

"Your wind's crummy," Leon told him.

"I've been a mess since my accident." Ritchie climbed in behind the wheel and they drove out of camp in low gear. The helibase was only a short drive to the north but the road was poorly graded and strewn with stones.

"Car accident?"

"Me and my old lady made eight grand last year at the Tok fire. Then she started sticking that coke up her nose and she pulled me out a window. Jeez, I don't even know what we were fighting about."

"You're lucky to be all right."

"Concussion, broken ribs. I was laid up for months."

Leon nodded and looked out the window.

"You putting in to Uncle Sam?" Ritchie said.

"What for?"

"This fire ends, we get laid off."

Leon grunted. Fighting wildfires was not something you got laid off from. The fires went out and there just wasn't any more work. "That must be union talk."

John Ritchie glanced at him and lit a cigarette.

The road was dusty, winding up the side of an old gravel pit. From the top they got a broad view of the burnt valley, a charred black landscape stretching below with rare islands of green foliage. Plumes of white smoke rose here and there and sometimes orange flames showed through the smoke.

The boys at the helibase helped them to unload the Ford. The supplies were laid in a cargo net spread open on the ground. In a minute a helicopter swooped down and hovered, and the boys went to work hooking up the net. Leon and John Ritchie turned back to base camp.

It was nearly four o'clock when they pulled in. They sat in the truck by the supply tent, John Ritchie saying that when he got off at four he would move his tent away from the pond or the mosquitos would never let him sleep. Across from them, the Tolmin crew sat among the supply boxes, looking hot and tired.

"Dumb Indians," Ritchie said.

Leon turned to him and caught a sharp whiff of sweat. "What's the use of talking like that?"

"Oh, sure, they'll put up a tent better than anybody, but watch when you turn your back, they'll up and quit."

"Is that where your Indian blood comes in?"

"Yeah, I got Indian blood," Ritchie said. "So?"

"Get some rest." Leon opened the door and stepped out. "You might rest better if you didn't smoke that shit on your break."

"Damn, how'd you know about that?"

"I know."

Ritchie reddened, studying his face. "Know what?"

"What d'you mean what? I smelled it."

"Oh." Ritchie spat out the window. "Yeah, I turned on the kid pretty good."

"Kid?" Leon stared into his eyes, then he looked over at Nelson sitting on one of the boxes with his legs drawn up, the red bandanna bright on his forehead. "That was Nelson and you in the woods?"

"What's it to you?"

"Get out of the truck."

John Ritchie got out of the truck and found a crowbar in the back. He came around to where Leon stood. "We got something to swing about, Leon?"

"They'll kick you out of firecamp for bringing that shit in."

"Why, someone tell on me?"

"He's too young for a scum like you to be fucking with."

"Fucking ain't half the wrong word," Ritchie said. He coughed his sickly cough and stared back at Leon. "Nelson's a grown man in case you didn't notice." He tucked the crowbar in his armpit, lit a cigarette and squinted over it. "I didn't force him, he came after me for it."

"I don't believe you."

"I'm telling you, he asked me for it."

Leon looked over at Nelson sitting there with the others of his village. Then he drew his fist back and hit John Ritchie in the mouth. Ritchie crumpled against the truck and as he dropped to his knees he swung the crowbar at Leon, then Leon kicked his boot in Ritchie's face and Ritchie spun in the dirt and lay there wheezing.

Leon stepped back. He hadn't expected to feel so angry, but he couldn't stand a mean-spirited lowlife like John Ritchie. The man had no principles. He made Indians look bad and he made white men look bad and he made everyone look bad but himself. Of himself he had a high enough opinion.

Ritchie sat up with his mouth all bloody and the supervisor came out of the supply tent and pulled Leon away. Leon looked over his shoulder for Nelson and saw a line of Athabaskan faces watching perplexedly, and he knew at that moment that tonight as surely as the black bear would return for the fatal bait, Nelson would wander through firecamp looking for John Ritchie's tent, and the two of them would make friends and talk and smoke and afterwards Nelson would stagger away through the bushes but tomorrow he'd be back.

Leon's shift lasted until midnight. It was a quiet time. A stakebed truck arrived at ten o'clock and Leon unloaded the supplies. The day was still light at their high latitude, but Leon built a fire to keep the mosquitos down, and the ranger came and sat with him awhile and talked about his family. Then around eleven-thirty the ranger returned to his truck for his shotgun and walked into the woods with it.

When the supervisor called Leon into the supply tent, it was to tell him what the IC had decided. Leon was being demobbed tomorrow because his conduct had violated firecamp rules. The supervisor apologized and Leon yawned and went outside.

The Indians were there, murmuring around their fire. Sometimes, like now during the summer, the piece of him that was theirs cried out a little louder than the rest of him, but he supposed if he was ever in Ireland the piece of him that was theirs would cry out a little louder too. What difference does it make? You've got to live your life, that's all. He had to look out better for himself. It was sweet having that swing at Ritchie, but that was no way to look out for himself—that swing beyond his control, born he didn't know where inside him, for no better reason than an Indian boy's youth.

Leon didn't sleep right away. In his tent he lay listening to the patter of mosquitos on the tent walls, the soft crunching of footfalls outside, the far, indistinct sounds of the woods. The night grew quieter, and it must have been one o'clock in the morning when a single gunshot echoed near the camp. Leon stared upwards for a moment, listening. Then it was quiet again and he turned over in his sleeping bag and went to sleep.

Naomi

The blue- and black-hulled boats jockey in their slips with a delightful idleness. The fleet has been asked to stand down and numbers of fishermen loiter on the docks of St. Paul Harbor with not much to occupy them while their representatives dicker with the canneries. In the light rain Tim Rafferty runs up to the harbormaster building to check the time on the public clock. It's half past two. As on the previous day, he finds himself drawn to the big hotel, and registers this fact with a stupid sort of awe, as if he hadn't all along been anticipating the hour when Naomi would come on duty.

Ducking his head in the rain, Tim tramps across gray Shelikof Street and with a quick step makes for the three-story hotel with the seven-ton anchor parked in front, considered by many to be the finest hotel in Kodiak.

The Lions Club has finished its weekly meeting down the hall. Tim, slumped in a chair in the hotel lobby, hears their muffled applause, and presently the members themselves file through the lobby. The sight of their well-dressed coterie, their self-satisfied faces, gets his back up, and he scowls into his magazine. At a few minutes past three Naomi comes in.

"You always look so happy," the receptionist calls to her.

"I drove through a huge pothole," Naomi reports with a shiver. Her hair is heavy and rain-darkened, and her smile turns the moment of fright into something sweet in recollection. "The whole car shook."

Tim, having risen to his feet, buries his hand in the soft fur of the stuffed musk ox beside him. Naomi is a tall girl with a sixteen-year-old's self-consciousness. She doesn't puff her chest out but guards her figure with an ungainliness that charms him. Her cheeks are ablaze with color.

"What will you draw today?" the receptionist asks her. This lady, not so humorless as she first appears, brightens in making her request. "Draw me a tiger?"

"A tiger!" Naomi sits behind the tour-booking desk and switches on the computer. She finds her sketch-pad in a drawer and opens it to a fresh page. "I'll try."

She acknowledges Tim's approach with a tremulous smile, dipping her head and averting her eyes until he has eased down in the chair across from her, a chair normally reserved for those hotel guests who seek her assistance in booking a bear-viewing flight or a fishing charter. In recent days anybody who noticed Tim Rafferty making free use of the washroom off the lobby, helping himself to the chocolate mints at the front counter, or beguiling the minutes in conversation with this pretty girl would have supposed him to be a lodger at the fine hotel. Sportsmen from foreign countries, big-city tourists, island residents just in from the bush—the hotel lodgers included every variety of humanity, and you can't easily judge a person by his rumpled clothes and his unshaved chin.

"Hi, Timothy. Are they still negotiating?"

"That's the word. There might be a strike vote."

Naomi nods her head in sympathy, but Tim has already seen how little she understands of the fishing business. Her father, himself a charter boat operator, a member of the local association that employs her to make bookings, must be a protective man indeed. Naomi knows nothing of the barnacled side of a boatman's life. Tim doubts she knows the difference between a captain and a capstan. Tim himself was a skipper at one time, fishing Dungeness crab and cod from his own boat, but more lately he is known as a capable hand on other men's salmon seiners. In this regard her ignorance is a mercy to him.

"I was thinking about something," he tells her. Philosophical impulses have stirred in him; he believes he has solved a riddle, or clarified a problem. "What you said yesterday, about love at first sight?"

"That we don't believe in it?"

"Yeah."

Her smile is bashful, but firm. "Because there's no such thing," she says.

"But what if the person was in your church?"

Naomi draws up one corner of her mouth. "That doesn't matter."

"If you meet a man who loves you and he wants to join your church?" Tim speaks quickly, fearing she won't understand him.

"It doesn't really change things," she says.

Tim is stunned by her reply. Surely he has penetrated to the crux of the problem. While he sits and ponders, Naomi searches up the internet image of a Bengal tiger, and, after silently contemplating the beast on her screen, a majestic cat with orange and black stripes, she opens her pencil box and begins to sketch it.

"Say he was to convert, or what you call it. They wouldn't let you?"

"Oh, you can marry, in a civil wedding. You're always free to do that. But it doesn't work."

"How do you know?"

"Look at the statistics. More than half the marriages..."

"I know about that," Tim grumbles.

Outside, the low white sky is undercut by the darkened street. Moisture bubbles the hotel doors and windows. The squall will blow itself out soon and he'll be left with the afternoon stretching before him. And with so little to choose from, really.

"Say she loves him back," he persists. "They love each other a lot."

"It doesn't last."

"How do you know?"

"Who somebody likes is based on their parents, media images, stuff like that. They light someone up. But it goes away."

Tim nods his head, weakly. Nothing else occurs to him to say. He becomes aware of the gentle, quick rasping of her pencil on the page. The fierce, expressive head, the thick neck and shoulder of a Bengal tiger take shape.

"What about friendship, children, stuff like that. It's not real?"

Her smile is shyly affirmative. "But it comes after marriage."

"But why can't it come after marriage to a person you love? If you've never even met a person..."

"You can find love in you for anybody."

"You can?"

"I see the kids at school, they don't even know what they're doing. Going on dates all the time, talking about their boyfriends." Naomi lowers her eyes and strikes her pencil across the page. "It's silly."

"Do you...do they tease you?"

"No. They don't bother me about it."

The way some people knit or shuffle cards or splice rope while they talk, Naomi sketches. Tim watches her and gulps with the mournful sense of her words. Cruel, it seems to him. The cruelest thing in the world. The foreclosure of everything hopeful about life. Not that he has any stake in Naomi's future but—what if he had? What if it was Tim Rafferty who loved her?

Inwardly he rages at an idea of love that seems perverted. It's grotesque, an old superstition someone has turned into a piety. She's in high school. Let her live!

But he has to admit she seems happy enough. Nothing in Naomi's appearance distinguishes her from other girls her age. Black denim pants worn low across her hips, a long-sleeved turquoise pullover. Her breasts are large; they bulk gently below the level of his eyes, adding to his sense of her awkward beauty. Her dark hair, pale skin, and the rich angles and depths of her face are the gifts of a Chinese mother and an Irish-Russian father who wedded eighteen years ago in Boston in a marriage arranged and administered by their church. They never even met before the ceremony. That Naomi's parents had never set eyes on each other before their wedding—to Tim it's a mystery, an astonishment, and frankly an insult.

"Listen," he has a sudden, sly thought. "What if you follow all the rules and your husband turns out to be a rotten apple? You're stuck with him, you can't divorce him," Tim leans forward in his chair, enjoying the moment of treachery, "he's terrible, he beats you..."

Naomi lowers her eyes in concession. "It's happened before. But I think..."

Tim scratches the red-gold hairs of his chin, waiting.

"I think I would try to help him."

"Help him! You mean cure him?"

She has a queer way of not quite looking at him, of ducking her head and furrowing the smooth white skin of her brow.

"The hardest thing is unselfishness," she says. "To think of others and not yourself. Should I sit down? Should I let someone else have the seat?" She laughs at herself and says, "It's really confusing. I catch myself being selfish all the time. It hurts my head. But when I try, I feel better. When I think about the good man."

"What good man?"

"The good man who's been through so much."

Tim has been listening to her with rising emotion. He gets to his feet, seeing a glimmer of hope for him in her code of unselfishness. He wants to argue love with her forever.

"We believe heaven is empty because no one is unselfish," she says.

These words have a crushing impact on Tim Rafferty. Nobody has ever talked to Tim about these things. Nobody ever talked to him about these things because nobody ever took him seriously enough. Her words are a scolding, a promise, a fire, an embrace, a salt bath, a body-and-soul shakedown. His throat is so inflamed, he can hardly speak.

"That's sad," he says.

"A little. But you have to try."

The receptionist calls to her from the front desk. "Room 205 is asking about a salmon/halibut combo. I told them to come down and see you."

"All right."

Tim has remained standing, leaning like a boat that has pulled up an overfull net. He twists around, the better to admire the tiger on Naomi's tablet. She arranges her colored pencils preparatory to using them. It amazes him how she can make something beautiful where there was nothing before, how she can populate a blank page with the life of the world.

"You're really good," he says.

"I always liked to draw."

"No, you've really got something. You have a gift."

Naomi looks up at him, touched by the strange insistence in his voice. They met three days ago after she noticed him mooning about the wood-paneled lobby and struck up a conversation with him. She loves to talk and she loves to sketch. During their brief acquaintance she has sketched all of the animal mounts displayed in the lobby—the elk, the musk ox and the brown bear. She enjoys it, but doesn't think much of her talent. "I look at it. I copy it."

Tim Rafferty sees otherwise. He's in the grip of a wild inspiration. Is there nothing he can do for her? He will help her to escape. The *Sea Queen,* he'll sell it for her, he'll kneel in front of her and beg her to take the money, all of it, and go somewhere, somewhere big, like Paris, or Rome, somewhere far from the block and tackle of a seagoing life, and use it, treat herself well, develop her specialness, paint vast animals on vaster canvases, and quakings and conjurings and weird flowerings like the one he's even now caught in the grips of but without having the tools to make sense of it for himself let alone erect into something he can hymn about forever, something that won't dribble out of his life again like water from the scuppers.

For just this rapturous moment Tim Rafferty forgets that he has no *Sea Queen* to sell anymore. That his boat and his crab pots and fishing gear have already fetched him forty grand and most of the money went to the IRS for penalty fees incurred by his wife before their divorce. That the *Sea Queen* later foundered in twenty-five-foot seas in the Shelikof Strait and one man went down with her. And that he has nothing else to offer this saintly girl, and she in all likelihood will go to some fellow who never before laid eyes on her but whose roll of the dice it will be to get her and to have her and to knock her up.

At the horror of this conception Tim balks. "Oh, God, I wish I'd never met you!" He bawls the words without shame because he is certain he will never see her again.

Tim's wheeling around causes a flutter in the little group of hotel guests standing nearby. Naomi blushes the deep pink color of a crab float and watches him run out the lobby door and into the world.

Cossacks

Lou married, and the notable thing about it is, he took his wife's name. Put it in the matrimonial records. His—you wouldn't call it maiden name—his handle as an unmarried man had been Bendler. What a relief to learn that Lou, the last holdout of their university crowd, had finally married and none of them was footloose anymore.

Just in your thirties you begin to wonder about the friends you've lost touch with. Lou found David's number on the internet and phoned him in March with news of the breakthrough. David was more moved than he could say.

"Bravo, my friend. Welcome to the life. When did this happen?"

There had been no wedding notice, no printed mementos. As for Lou's taking his wife's name, David didn't know of this until a letter came from Lou in mid-summer asking if the invitation to visit them in Alaska was still open.

"You bet, Lou." David phoned him in California. "You'll bring your bride?" The years in the North had isolated David from his old friends, he confessed this to Lou in as many words. "You'd be doing me a favor to come. And Katie would love to meet her."

So Lou's doubts were disposed of. "But I'm coming alone," he said.

"What about September?"

"If I can shake free of the office."

"There's no better month for grouse. Still want to try it?"

"David, I haven't got a gun."

"Leave it to me, chum."

It's Kate who brings the conspicuous but over-looked detail to David's attention, the name *Lou Hickey* printed on the return address label. "Look," she taps her finger on the envelope after David has hung the phone up. "I thought his name was Bendler."

"So did I." David cocks his eye at the label, his eye-brows alternately plunging and rising. By God, she was right. "Lou Hickey!"

A fit of laughter comes over them. "And a million-aire to boot," he says. They become frisky, he chases her around the dining room. "You won't poke fun when he's here?"

"You know I won't," she says.

"Promise?"

She drags the chairs into his path. "I promise."

"What guts," he says. "Women should lift him on their shoulders and take him to town. Gotcha!"

He swings her around. The color has risen in Kate's cheeks, but her face is downcast.

"You would never have done it for me," she says.

"Done what?"

"Change your name."

"Would you want me to?"

"David, I asked you to."

"I guess I'm not strong enough."

"What has strength got to do with it?"

"Go on, change it back," he says. "I didn't make you."

Her eyes fill with tears. "We're a family, David."

"Katie..."

But she has turned her back. "Lou's Jewish, isn't he?"

"Twice the Jew I am, which isn't much of one. Why?"

"Is that a Jewish name?"

"Hickey? It sounds cosmopolitan to me."

Their boy cries out in his sleep, and Kate turns her head and listens. David rubs her shoulder and she relaxes. They married after college, honeymooned to Alaska, and settled here. How much of a woman he was getting ten years ago and didn't know it. In those days it would never have occurred to him to see her as a Christian woman strapping a Jewish name on her back, voluntarily and for life—forever!

"I know what you're thinking, Kate."

"What?"

"That Lou Hickey rhymes with doohickey."

She wheels around, clenching her jaws so as not to laugh at him. "Damn you," she says. She slaps him so hard it feels like a saucepan hitting him.

"Is this from your self-defense class? Let go."

She stalks away—it angers him. "Expect me tonight, Kate."

"Not for a year," she says.

"I'll work my way up."

"No, you're no good anyway."

"Who taught me?" he says. "Cheek to the comb, firm grip, controlled breathing," he runs after her, "bango!"

Kate is as good as her word: the house receives Lou as one of its own. "No shoes in the house is her only rule, Lou. Especially not those godawful preppy things."

They embrace under the stuffed moose head by the baggage carousel at Fairbanks International. It's Sunday.

"Your own office on Ocean Avenue," David scolds him, "that's no excuse for letting yourself run down."

Lou narrows his eyes. "What's different about you, David? Your hair?"

"My hair's longer. I'm not a virgin. I know what indigestion is. I quit smoking. I'm a father. I understand the class system better. I could go on. You?"

David feels strangely romantic, seeing Lou again, this fellow of his youth, his cousin in time. He wants everything to be just right for him. If things go well, then the past is still on course. In college they were friends, David irrepressible, Lou a glum cynic, David a poet, promiscuous in slipping the fruits of his art under women's doors, Lou a shuffling professor's boy, bemoaning life's dullness. How good to hear that Lou had made a mint!

Katie knew him in school but not well. They moved in different social circles. She recalls a certain dorkiness in Lou. Dorky, no, but Lou was always paunchy, true, he's shaped like a big soft wineskin. It's the same old Lou. Bulky, pallid. Tortoiseshell eyeglasses. Today at his wages they're probably real tortoiseshell.

Lou speaks matter-of-factly about the millions of dollars he juggles for his living. "The way the economy's been, any fool could have done it." Investment broker. His own office in Santa Monica. Tentacles in New York. At first David is abashed for him. He's bragging to me! Showing off to a woodcutter! No, that's not it. To Lou, he's still David, the David lacking in mercenary good sense. Lou is being honest. And David is glad for him. With friends of your youth, that's how it is: ten years' clutter gone, wiped out.

After lunch Lou tours the property. "Our estate," David calls it, extending his arms. Autumn has wreaked its usual havoc on the vegetable world. Woody shrubs and herbs all intertwined in a last hurrah. Dew saturates their shoes and pantlegs as they smash through the tangles. Kate and Joni hold hands, mother and daughter hiking abreast where the trail permits, bursting through the briers and saplings, the rose hips raking their sides.

Six of the ten acres are wooded. "Another fifteen grand and it's ours," David says. Little Ben rides on his back, asleep in the carrier. Lou plods heavily, but lightens on his toes with each step. "It's beautiful," he murmurs. "Beautiful."

Joni, conquering her shyness, offers rotted raspberries to the visitor, the bright juice running down her fingers.

"David's wood lot," Kate announces.

Red gas cans and white oil jugs lie tipped on their sides. The wood lot is inches deep in sawdust and moldering bark chips. Lou trundles to the far side and sends a hoist chain swinging into the wall of a storage crib. Everything is so alien to him, he turns up his hands, made mute by the strangeness of it. Cordwood is stacked by age and by kind. A truck is backed up, a load of logs lashed to its flat bed.

"It's all birch and spruce," David explains. "Smart people use birch, but everybody loves a spruce fire."

David is licensed to harvest surplus wood from state land, but he's not above poaching beetle-killed trees from outside his permit area.

They emerge on the lawn and linger in silence. Yellow leaves strew the grass. The screen house, erected by David each summer, octagonal in shape, with a peaked vinyl roof patterned in alternating triangles of green and white, and flanked by two chokecherry trees, stands midway on the lawn between them and the family house. Masses of frost-hardy columbine survive in the flower beds, the pink and white bells rollicking in the face of the coming cold.

"I've stopped mowing for the year," David says, toeing the tousled grass. "Too wet. Sun can't keep up with it."

"It's all so lovely," Lou says.

"Dad?" Joni has taken his hand.

"Sweetheart?"

Below in the driveway, a raven is feeding on some offal it has found, and every few seconds it beats its wings and jumps into the air, croaking irately at the cat Cloud who makes an amusement of stalking the bird.

"Why don't we eat people we don't like?" she says.

"Hm? Hoooo!" David considers his daughter's question, kneeling beside her and gazing down the driveway, enjoying the softness of her cheek against his own. "Wow, that's a toughie. Well, some people do, sweetheart. But not very many these days. Besides, I don't think people would taste very good, do you? I wouldn't worry about it."

In the guest room the Gideon Bible on the bedtable sends Lou over the edge. His belly shakes with laughter, his snorts are like sausage casings ripping open.

"Take your sweater off, Lou, relax." David swats the bed and with a grand sweep of his arm tears down the mosquito netting. "The bugs are gone, it's one of the bounties of the season. There's booze on the dresser. Towels. You want something, just ring."

"Thanks, David."

"It's the least I can do. Everything okay?"

"Sure."

"Is it too early to harangue you for not bringing your wife?"

"We needed some time," Lou says.

"Already?"

"Already."

"Are you hunting with my dad tomorrow?"

It's Joni. She's been following them.

Lou, thirty-two years a city boy, looks at David's three-year-old daughter, embarrassed by her question. Haw-haw, he guffaws. It frightens her off.

David muses, watching her go. "Tomorrow she starts preschool. Kate thinks it's better if she's not in her class, but...It's a new world for her."

"Everybody grows up, David."

"Yes, so they say."

The thought occurs to David that, with the Montessori opening tomorrow and Kate's summer vacation come to an end, she might be in an untamable funk this evening and he had better keep an eye on her. Not that anything will hold Kate back if she decides to lash out. As regards Lou and his recent marriage, Kate could be either cutting or charitable, depending on her mood. In the end she chooses the way of tact and understanding. In fact she's almost too polite. In conversation they refer to the detail of Lou's taking his wife's name, but only abstractly, without sounding out Lou's deepest feelings about it, as if it were no radical departure but a mere curiosity. To the question *What's in a name?* there are, they decide, two answers: *It doesn't matter* and *A lot*. In some cultures a woman keeps her family name, the children take their mother's name, and so on. But apart from the anthropology of it, to David and Kate it seems somehow indelicate on the first night of Lou's visit to ask him outright why he did it—took his wife's name, turned the tradition on its head—has he been tormented for it? does he regret it? and so on.

After dinner, after the children have gone to bed, the evening being fair, though cool, they pull on their sweaters and jackets and carry their wine outside, across the lawn to the screen house between the choke-cherry trees. Here, at the round, glass-topped table, they sip their wine and exchange memories of their college years, and through the lens of time are able to regard past agonies as blessings and to see conceitedness for the vanity it is. The summer's end hasn't piqued Katie as David feared that it might, but adds to the atmosphere of tender forgiveness that rules their reunion, and they guard as precious these moments in which a warmth has sprung up in defiance of the season.

"I only wish your wife were here too," Kate says.

"She's running it while I'm gone. Finances, personnel, everything. She's very good. I've no complaints."

"Next time."

"Yes, next time."

The sour, woodsy smell of highbush cranberry wafts through the mesh of the screen walls. In the late twilight they watch a robin devour what few choke-cherries cling to the twigs of the branches. David trots back to the house for the dinner wine, and before returning he switches on the halogen yardlight, and doesn't neglect to bring his guitar with him.

"...too risky," Kate is telling Lou. "If we don't know the mother, if she has a different last name from her child and she comes to pick the child up early, we turn her away. It happened several times last year."

"That's terrible," Lou says.

"I asked David to change his name but he wouldn't."

"Lou," David interjects, strumming his guitar, "if there's one thing that's kept me from roaming out of bounds in my marriage, it's Kate's taking my name. She knows this. If I betray her, I betray myself."

Lou smiles at Kate. "He knows what to say."

"No, I mean it," David says. "A piece of my heart. But look, do you see what I mean? I've no sooner slipped away—All they want to do is fight fight fight with us. *There was a girl in Memphis...*"

"The statistics look good for women," Lou says.

"What statistics are you talking about?" Kate says.

"If we don't evolve together, we're not evolving," David says. "That's by definition. We come to the promised land together. Let's have some morale please! I don't understand people who frame progress in terms of victory and defeat. Look at the vistas open to us if we seized them."

A follower of the stock market, Lou is alarmed by David's oratory. In reaction he cozies up to Kate with a fatuous grin on his face. "David has a passionate nature."

"Europeans believe that American men are browbeaten," Kate observes.

What a thing to say to a man who's just been grinning at you like a spaniel! "At least she doesn't call us pussy-whipped," David says. "But frankly that's a French specialty. Look, speaking of Europe, I'm saying bulls aren't gentled with banderillas. Stick them, they get angry."

"If history is ending, as some people say, then the battle of the sexes will go the way of bullfighting," Kate says.

"That's a laugh," David says. "Wait, I've hit on something. Most bulls don't even make it into the ring, isn't that the point? It's supposed to be an honor."

"This is coming from a man whose favorite book is *Ferdinand the Bull*," Kate says.

"A congresswoman talks in military metaphors, she's read an ancient Chinese manual on succeeding in politics and we're all so impressed," David says. "What an advance! Then you have these ideologues that get their jollies by poisoning young people's innocent courtships just because they never knew romantic happiness themselves and can't bear that anybody else should."

Kate passes her empty glass to David, who reaches across his guitar and fills it from the spigot of the five-liter wine box.

"Lou, I'm only afraid you'll wish you hadn't done it," David says. "A nail sticks out, people take a hammer to it. I hope I'm wrong." And he strums his guitar singing

> *There was a girl in Memphis*
> *(and I don't mean Tennessee)*
> *with breasts like topless pyramids,*
> *and I sat on her knee.*
>
> *A wonder is a wonder,*
> *and I so newly swaddled*
> *would gladly from those tits have drunk,*
> *but I got only bottled.*

David has eight basic chords and he sticks with them, sometimes kicking off a measure with a bass note or trilling an arpeggio just to show his derring-do.

"Did Christo or Oldenburg or any of those artists do the Pyramids yet?"

"Which pyramids?"

"Napoleon did the Pyramids."

"Besides Napoleon."

"Hmm..."

"What about the painter—the one that's really good at tits."

"Which one?"

"Which one? The left one. No, it starts with a W. Or is it H?"

"All painters are good at tits. That's all they're good at."

> *They shipped him down the river course*
> *in a coracle of grass,*
> *and there tossed on the river bank*
> *the babe beshat his ass.*
>
> *They picked him up and hugged him close*
> *and swabbed his little bum:*
> *"Oh look," they cried, "it's circumcised!"*
> *And thence the word was mum.*

"David."

"Hm?"

A wind has come up, stirring the leaves of the birch trees. To east an enormous harvest moon has risen over the treetops. David and Katie smile at each other with the unconscious rudeness of lovers much younger than themselves. He goes to the kitchen and returns carrying an old-fashioned salver with bottles on it of Bailey's, Kahlúa, Amaretto and Frangelico arranged like four angels around three cordial glasses.

"The children..."

"Are fine," he says. "The nights are getting dark. Your health, everybody."

The arc of grass illuminated by the yardlight extends almost as far as the screen house. The soft light slips down the stems of their drinking glasses. They talk well into the night, the three friends, hardly noticing how with the passing minutes the first tentative gusts of wind grow into a continuous stream that blows around the screen house and through its mesh walls. The tops of the trees sway in the wind and soon the trunks themselves bend and creak. The sky shrinks and darkens, and in short order the tight mass of clouds that has skated in on the wind is hiding the moon and showering rain on them.

The rain drums on the vinyl roof of the screen house. The overhanging edges of the roof buckle in the drafts, scattering streams of raindrops. Branches clash, plastic toys skitter across the lawn, and the chains of the swingset flash and jingle. Lou, tightening his collar, David protectively hugging his guitar, and Kate as smoothly upright as the bottles on the tray she carries, they hasten back to the house, calling to one another and jesting as they go.

After midnight the clouds disperse, passing over the country. The night is clear, and every leaf falling in the woods casts a shadow in the moonlight.

In the morning David and Lou drive the pickup truck south on the Parks Highway past Skinny Dick's, the inn across the road from where the record black bear was shot in '96. It's the hour when the mist is rising from the lakes and ponds and there isn't any traffic on the road. They share coffee from a Thermos and eat bran muffins from a brown bag propped on the seat between them.

"There was no extravaganza," Lou says. "We hardly told anyone. I only thought of you afterwards."

"That's how people do it nowadays."

"No, we're going to have a family. She was already pregnant."

"I see. It's no big deal. But Lou, that's great."

"Yeah." He gives a flatulent laugh, shifting in the seat.

"Where does that put her?"

"Three months to go."

"Terrific."

"David..."

"She's big?"

Lou makes no answer, staring out the window at the yellow aspens.

"You big oaf, what is it? Some rocky moments? She won't jerk you off even? What's wrong?"

"I waited too long maybe. Set in my ways."

"Katie puked every day for nine months. Give me a break. You think it's easy for them?"

"I think I'm supposed to be happier."

"Happy!" Braking hard, David throws the steering wheel to the left and turns the truck off the road.

"Whoa, David."

"This is my favorite spot. Get out."

"What, here?"

David jumps out of the truck, thinking: He's the same, the same as ever, a moper, bemoaning his lack of fulfillment in life. What should I tell him? What's the cure for the self-image of a jelly-bellied city Jew? A fine bust in the rogue's gallery of the high bourgeois and grudging himself every minute of it.

"Understand something, Lou," David yells over his shoulder as he pees into the roadside fireweed, "you're not going to get it as often as you like. It's up to you to make clear your minimum. Don't let it hang, I warn you. On a personal note I find I'm most satisfied when I'm thinking of my wife. Try it. The wonder is she wants a pig like you at all."

Being around Lou sends college-era words flitting through his head. *Eudemonics...entelechy...*What a lot of bullshit. The words offend him now. But he's troubled. What is it his friend needs? If you could call regret one of the aims and pleasures of life, here was his friend Lou Hickey (born Bendler) stifled in his pursuit of it—yes, positively stinking of unrealized regret, unrealized because his life wouldn't permit him genuine regret, since all the evidence was against him. "Your life is good, Lou," life kept telling him, again and again, and Lou refused to believe it.

Everything decent in life was his, all the grounds for contentment—education, health, money, success, friends, peace in the land, a woman's companionship. But it was all a burden, to hear him tell it. You wouldn't envy his money even. From a life so blatantly blessed, what's missing? Is it the adventure, the suffering, the hardship he hankers for, the thing that makes him read biographies of Sir Richard Burton, the journals of the explorers, and loathe himself for not having the courage, chutzpah, guts, balls, gusto, whatever you want to call it, to do deeds as bold and bloody and momentous as these men, to trace a river to its source, to rip the quavering heart out of life itself and raise it to his lips?

And this is what he comes up with? How a conventional man courts the unconventional these days? By taking his wife's name? David puts up his zipper.

"If you have to ask if you're happy, Lou, you've got your answer already."

"Why? What's wrong with asking? Everybody wants it. It's normal, it's human."

"If you put it up on the mantel like something a kid pines to reach, forget it."

"You never ask yourself if you're happy? I don't believe it. You're afraid of the word, David."

This pining of well-fed people for the idol of happiness makes David revolt. But it's true he once in a desolate hour, staring at hands he couldn't believe had been made to be so calloused and cracked and filthy, resolved that his only true failure in life would be not to be happy. Behind such a resolve's an idea of happiness. How convenient then never to hold it up to see how reality agrees with it. Lou's words are full of stingers.

"Contentment, well-being, happiness," Lou presses him. "You're only shifting the burden from one word to another."

"Some things don't fit in words," David says. They're standing on the road shoulder overlooking the valley of the Tanana River. David draws the air into his lungs, and the beauty of the vista, of the river valley and the snow peaks in the distance, sets up a fine trembling in his torso.

"What's wrong?" Lou says.

"Nothing. Don't you recognize it?"

Lou nods over the valley. "I'm looking, I'm looking."

"It's the background from the *Mona Lisa*."

"I...see what you mean," Lou says.

"You're blind, Lou. Happiness is grace, it's bounty. It's free of charge, it's given to you. You don't win it. You don't earn it. You don't deserve it. You say yes. You just say yes." David has raised his voice, he all but grabs Lou by the chest and shakes him, and Lou steps back in astonishment. A car speeds by on the highway, the driver glances out at them on the roadside. Beyond them the Tanana River meanders in its shimmering course over miles of smoky blue flatlands. Deep green spruce forests roll down to the banks and recede, and the hardwood stands make a patchwork of autumn colors muted in the early light. A bluish haze envelops the land but even at a distance the reticulations of individual trees are visible. The smooth surface of the river absorbs the pallor of the sky and flows on. All through the valley, plumes of mist rise from the ponds and muskegs.

"The grouse are getting their grits," David says. "Let's go."

"You really think Leonardo...?"

"I'm sure of it. He came in one of his flying machines and got home before anyone knew he was gone."

They drive south a few miles and turn left off the highway. A dusty road leads down a steep wooded grade. On both sides the leaves color the air with as bright a yellow as children paint in primary schools. Lou rolls up his window against the dust.

"Down there's an old burn," David says. "Late October, our first year in Fairbanks, we drove here to cut firewood, Katie and me, we lost it on the ice—nearly slid off the edge. Pretty steep, huh? There goes an old logging road. Good grouse country."

David at the wheel, Lou bouncing beside him, they descend into a vast clearing, the pickup truck lurching over rotted, moss-grown stumps, willow saplings thrashing the bumpers and running boards.

"Six grand in a new red Samurai and a bunch of school loans, that's all we had," David recalls. He stops the truck and they get out. Brambles and charred rampikes mark the waste around them. A belt of old conifers curves down the slope to their right and mixes with the yellow hardwoods below. Water glints at the base of the hill where a creek flows among the alder thickets and cottonwoods, one of the innumerable waterways that feed the Tanana River.

"We'll head for those woods," David prods Lou into motion. "Mixed areas like this are good. Watch for berries. Go on, there's no snakes in Alaska. You ever read Jack London? Ho, what a naturalist! Check your safety. What are those boots?"

"L.L.Bean."

They hike briskly to ward off the chill, dressed in light jackets and loose trousers. David wears a knapsack filled with gear. They both carry guns.

"We might find them in coveys at this time of year. If it's a wingshot, you'll have two seconds max."

"This is funny," Lou says.

"Laugh, it might flush a bird."

Lou does laugh—a honking, clumsy laugh, looking through his eyeglasses at David. "It's strange, that's all. What am I doing here?"

"Filling a hole in yourself. Moving on to the next best thing. Cutting the last apron string. I had to teach myself, you know. My old man shot guns in the army, but he never hunted."

"I don't know, David."

"It's good for you. You're a snob. Did you tell me your people were German?"

"Mmhm. What about you?"

"The Russian hinterlands somewhere. Cossack country. I imagine a certain Count Fukhov whose estate we lived in the shadow of. One day my mother was taking water from the well..."

When they fall silent, David cracks sticks between his hands to make noise. They push far into the woods, the damp leaves muffling their footsteps. Overhead, the yellow leaves are so plentiful, it's impossible to believe the trees will ever be bare of them.

Their path dips and rises, winding among hollows of willow and brier and cranberry. Alder-filled trenches cut this way and that. Mushrooms swell in the soil.

"You'll be awkward with your newborn same as that shotgun, Lou. But you'll get used to it. The feeling of holding a three-day-old baby to your chest!" David stops in the trail and shuts his eyes, cradling in his arms his .22-caliber rifle. It's a gesture Lou refuses to take seriously.

"You're joking, David."

"A balm for the heart. It's my one regret about not making more money. Katie can't afford to quit even if she wanted. I wouldn't stop with two, believe me. You and Mrs. Hickey should get busy."

They have hardly resumed their hike before a grouse thunders into the air to their left. The sudden beating of wings so startles them, neither man collects himself in time to raise his gun.

David drops to his belly, watching the blur of its flight through the branches.

"A ruffed grouse." He jumps to his feet. "Come on."

A minute later they huddle panting thirty yards shy of the tree in which the grouse perches. The white of its breast feathers blends so well with the white of the birch bark, it's only the contrast of gray wings and yellow leaves that gives it away.

"Gets your heart going, huh? Go on."

Hesitating, Lou ventures forward. The grouse clucks and shifts on its branch, made uneasy by Lou's approach. The bird worries it has been discovered and betrays itself by its jitters. Lou stares dolefully into the tree and lifts his shotgun with exaggerated deliberateness. He stretches out his neck, lays his cheek to the gun's comb, sights up the length of the barrel, and does it with such admirable determination, makes such a production of it that the grouse, now fully alarmed, raises its crest feathers.

The bird spreads its wings and has left its branch before the shot rings out. The report resounds through the woods and the grouse drops fifty feet through the center of it. Yellow leaves swirl in the air. White feathers drift down after it.

"Was it difficult, Lou?"

Lou nods his head, looking down at the bird.

"Listen," David tells him, "they have those hoity-toity black-tie dinners for five hundred bucks a plate, this is what they're served, the lousy hypocrites—a ruffed grouse. Don't feel bad. Go on, pick it up. Let's bag some grouse."

Late in the afternoon, after having hiked several miles by the creek and wound uphill among the trees, they reemerge in the clearing carrying game bags stained red from the carcasses inside. Between them they have killed eleven grouse. Their cheeks are bright with color, they have stripped down to their t-shirts, it was a fine day and they never even stopped to eat their sandwiches.

"Tomorrow, if you don't want to powder 'em, if they stand there clucking like that nitwit of a spruce hen, try it with my .22 if you want, that's what it's for," David says. "Or throw a rock, it spooks them."

"I can hear people saying bad things about me."

"So?" David sets his game bag on a log in front of the pickup truck, opens it, looks at the birds inside, heaves a sigh of satisfaction, then sits with his back to the log and gazes out over the expanse of deciduous trees and the creek far below.

"We get a short autumn here. The leaves'll fall in torrents. If you want, we'll hunt all week. I'm glad you came, Lou."

Lou sits down beside him. "What about Katie?"

"What I'm selling this year had better be seasoned by now anyway. Another couple of weeks I'll be swamped with deliveries. I can cut green wood any time." He upends his knapsack and dumps its contents on the ground between his outstretched legs.

"How much money do you make at it?"

"Ten grand a year roughly. A hundred cords. I'll buck it for nothing but there's a surcharge for delivery." He picks through his gear: a folding knife, a box of grouse shells, a box of .22s, half a dozen big-game slugs, an empty water canteen, a rag, plastic bags, four squashed sandwiches, and a silver flask. "Besides, if we run into a bull moose, the week pays for itself." He swigs from the polished flask, then leans toward Lou looking closely at his neck. "What's that?"

"What?"

"On your neck."

"I don't know."

"It's a hickey, Lou."

"Very funny."

"Why'd you do it?"

"She asked me would I. I love her."

"That much," David says.

"Sure."

"But Hickey!"

Lou grunts. "I can afford it."

"Did she make an ultimatum?"

"No, nothing like that."

"You're a trailblazer. I wouldn't have the guts."

"Guts?" Lou considers the word. "Something happens when a pile of money falls in your lap, David. You get impulsive. And with women...well, you never know."

David hands him the flask. "Your pop take it standing up?"

"He complains. It's his hobby since he retired." Lou steams from the mouth, lowering the flask. "Wow."

"They're still picking over the corpse of the Soviet empire. That was a gift to me. It came from a catalog, a very fashionable one I might add."

Lou studies the Cyrillic letters engraved on the flask bottom. "Whose was it?"

"Some officer's maybe. An antique."

"CCCP."

"That's Russian for RIP."

Lou unscrews the cap on which Vladimir Lenin is cameoed in gilt on red enamel and downs another slug before returning the flask to David.

"It's ironic," Lou says. "Your Katie, she takes your name, and you..."

"I what? Hunt grouse and make ten grand a year?" David chuckles, resting his hand on Lou's shoulder. "You, you're a millionaire, you could've bought yourself a Barbie doll."

"When are you going to get serious, David?"

"Huh?"

"And come to your senses."

David draws back from him. "I'm surprised at you."

"Sure, I can do this for a week," Lou says, "I'm refreshed, I feel strong, but...You can buy chicken in the store you know. You're no killer, David."

"What do you mean by that?"

"It's your life I'm talking about."

"It's not so complicated. We go home. I cook the ruffs for us. I play with the children. Caress Katie's forehead. She eases my conscience two-three times a week. I let her beat me up if she wants. Winter I dance in the snow while my daughter waves at me through the window. Katie does what she wants. She happens to like teaching school. I'm lucky. We've enough to live on, we love each other. We don't pay a dime for meat or fish. There's people that can't stand it, I know. Everyone but the paraplegics is in harness these days. Look, he's goofing off! It drives them nuts. Guys have hit on her, they say they want to take care of her better than her husband does. Sure, she tells me. In a town like this, I know them, I'd spit on them in the street if I wasn't so ashamed for them. Married guys! God save her for being true to me. And if she hasn't, well, God save me from knowing it. Look at this..."

David rises to his feet, gesturing at the autumn blaze of the trees, the creek spinning down the valley floor. "It was put here for all of us, Lou. I've made the voyage, I'm here, you see. You think after all these years I don't take it seriously?" He sips from his flask, the sky a deep, cloudless blue overhead. More than any argument, it's the beauty of the vista that moves him. The air cycles in and out, and at the top of each cycle, when his lungs are their fullest, he feels as big as the sky.

"The grouse were here before the priests came along, Lou. You think Count Fukhov hanged poachers only because he hated thieves? For that matter, why do so many educated snobs hate this sport of ours? Think about it, my friend. Think good and hard. What's it all about?"

The white florets of wild yarrow bump against his thighs. His old blue polypropylene t-shirt is stained dark with spruce gum. "Power," he says. Until now David has spoken mildly, but when he turns on Lou he is suddenly vehement. "Power. It's about power," he says. "You think it doesn't piss 'em off there's a couple of yids running free at the top of the world shooting the wild game for their messes?"

"Take it easy, David. I didn't mean that."

They hear the whisper of water flowing down the creek at the base of the hill. Across the valley the slopes are banded with the bright colors of the passing foliage, the hardwood trees making yin and yang with the stands of dark conifer. From over their shoulders the sun lights the woodlands below, and sometimes in the breeze a canopy of golden leaves flutters and an intricate brilliance is set in motion. Then the scattered notes of the birds join in evening song and the tangy breath of the fall touches their faces. On some of the trees the flanking leaves have already coppered. The crowns of the aspens flame bright red.

And something happens to David as he gazes on this splendor. It's like a blow to his midriff that rises with a jolt through his body and presses out through his eyes. He nods uncontrollably, as if he were ill.

"There's just no arguing against the world at a time like this, Lou. It's too beautiful. It's like the late-season bloom on a wild rose. There's always one, you know. What if everybody felt this way? No, but I know, no—it can't work, I'm no rabbi or priest, I'm no anchorman or vice chairman or anything important like that. Anyway, I don't care about that either, I..."

"David, come back here. Sit down."

"I'm sorry. We'll breast these birds, huh? Let's see what's in the gizzard. Where's my knife? I can already tell you, it's cranberries and willow shoots. A stuffed ruff, ha! Some left in the flask, want it?"

Just as David eases down by Lou, a grouse flies out of the spruce grove uphill of them and dips over their clearing. Its foreshortened wings, its plump brown contours are unmistakable, and David, as he sits, grabs up the long-barreled shotgun. Rocking back, he swings the gun up and, following on the flare of the grouse's tail, touches off a shot. It knocks the bird from the air.

"Look at that," David says. He lays the gun aside and drinks what's left in the flask. "I didn't think I'd get him."

"You!" Lou is suddenly mirthful, his eyes sparkle with amusement. "Look at yourself, David."

"What?"

"You've turned Cossack on us, that's what."

"This?" David rattles the flask. "It's tin."

"No, not that. It's everything about you, David. You're happy enough, why hide it? Why deny it?"

"Happiness?"

The word, when he has spoken it, releases something in David, thoughts and feelings pent up or long concealed in him, and a blur of names and faces flits unbidden through his mind. It's the roster of a family that is practically lost to him, hapless faces and fearful faces and faces lively with irrational good cheer, the faces of penniless wanderers, tradesfolk and city professionals, all of whose dreams he inhabits—David sees this in a flash—and sees, too, that for as long as he fulfills his obligations to those who have dreamed him—lives his life as freely and fully as they could only have dreamed of doing—then nothing, nothing on earth can harm him.

Not more than a second passes in this reflection. A feverish excitement, a heady sort of wonder comes over David. "Happy?" He turns to Lou. "Sure, why not? Hands down. No holds barred," he says.

Lou laughs aloud, he fires his shotgun in the air. "Take that!" Smoke curls from the muzzle, he lets off a second round. It roars over the valley, the leaves do extra spirals in the air.

"Take that, you Cossacks!"

David laughs too, crossing his arms and leaning back against the log. He gazes across the valley, a serene smile on his face, thinking, This is for the rag men and the seamstresses and the numbskull ironmongers. For the failed insurance men, the suicides, and the harried professors caught in the crossfire. For them that never knew the compass in their lives of a day of peace and leisure. Nothing beats it.

Caribou, Paxson Lake

She tossed the bent oar down between their packs and drew her arms inside her dripping raincoat while he undid the red and black wires of the electric motor and hauled the battery out after it.

"The damn thing. I should have known better."

"Where are we?" she said.

"East side of the lake." They were both breathing hard. "Give me a hand."

They dragged the boat up on the shore and turned it over to let it drain. He held her in his arms. "You all right?"

"You said the battery was good for six hours."

"I know what I said."

"What should we do?"

"Slow down a minute." He looked back at the boiling lake surface. They had been out in the middle of the lake when the battery cut out. The rain fell hard and the wind was blowing and their twelve-foot inflatable pitched up and down in the waves. He had unclamped the motor from the transom to keep the dead propeller from dragging in the water and while his back was turned the port oar got wrenched in its oarlock; it was hollow aluminum and bent irreparably. That was the crippled state they finally made shore in.

"I didn't think Paxson Lake would blow up like this," he said.

"Big lakes do. I don't blame you."

"It's nothing but a light trolling motor." He helped her on with her pack. "We shouldn't have been out there."

"A poor man's hunt," she said. She slid her hand up the barrel of his rifle and flung the water off it. "What do you want to do?"

He had wanted to be at the south end of the lake by now. They had planned to leave the boat at the mouth of the Gulkana River and from there to climb west into higher country where they would be in a position to glass for caribou and to shoot one in the morning. The legal hunt opened at midnight.

"We won't make the opening," he said.

"How far down the lake are we?"

"There's a ways to go."

"Well, we can't swim across. There's no point in going back yet."

He caught her by the arm. "You looked so small, kneeling in the bow."

"You were worried about me."

"Of course."

They left the boat behind, hiking to the south, but as they talked they kept returning to the experience.

"Why didn't you tell me sooner?" she said.

"Didn't want to alarm you."

"Alarm me! The shape of the mountain never changed. It seemed like eternity."

"You knew we were in trouble."

"I knew you'd gotten quiet."

They were in an excitable state, they couldn't leave it alone. They followed an animal trail south around the lake and found plenty of caribou sign—droppings, tracks in the mud where the moss was worn away, but their thoughts kept returning to the boat.

"There was nothing in front of me," she said. "Just those dark swells."

"What were you thinking?"

"The kids."

"Of course, the kids."

"I'm sorry for saying what I said."

"What did you say?"

"About the poor man's hunt."

"Between the kids and the money, there's no other kind," he said.

It was late afternoon in the foothills of the Alaska Range. Cold, drippy and overcast, it felt more like the first of October than the middle of August. But there were flowers growing, aster and parnassus and many monkshood on the thin trails that braided the mossy grades of the lakeside. The rain had fallen steadily all day. Low mists obscured the opposite shores of the lake. The twilight cast mulberry shadows.

The next creek crossing particularly vexed them. At the mouth of the creek, the shore dropped too steeply to let them wade the lake shallows without flooding their hip boots. The creek itself ran deep in its channel and was shouldered by quicksand, pale, deceptive, silted mud that grabbed the leg of his hip boot the way a wall holds a toggle bolt that's been opened behind it.

"Son of a bitch. I'm not in a mood to chance this."

They hiked up the creek until they found a suitable crossing, then redescended to the lake, a detour of forty-five minutes.

The weather was miserable. He knocked the water off his hatbrim, peering down the lake in the fog. She watched the rain flowing into his rifle barrel and, reaching over, tipped the gun down. Love, she reflected. There's always love. Get his mind off the damn boat. Love is something a woman has up her sleeve without deluding herself about the source of its magic. What he really needed was to come out of the hunt with a caribou.

"How high are we?" she said. "I'm dizzy."

"Dig the GPS out, we'll see." He turned his back so she could get into the side pocket of his backpack.

"Let's stop and make camp," she said.

He stayed quiet long enough to communicate his disappointment but not so long as to blame her. Her raincoat clung to her and she was thoroughly soaked; he leaned back and laughed at her. "We'll stop."

"If the weather improves, we'll start first thing, I promise," she said.

At this time of the year the caribou would be dispersed, especially given the lousy weather. The Richardson Highway passed east of them, closer than he liked, but there wouldn't be any hunting pressure in the storm. "It's too open here," he said. "Let's get off the watering hole." He nodded up the hill, beyond the point where they had crossed the creek. "There's a good view up top."

"You don't mind?"

"I don't mind." He took an altitude reading with the GPS set, her recent birthday gift to him. "Twenty-five hundred feet."

"Maybe the herd will come through."

"In snot like this, I doubt it."

They looked up the hill together.

"Well, longjohns and brandy," she said.

They climbed among the spruce trees that dotted the lakeside, their footfalls muffled by the moss and by the immense but subtle timbre of the raindrops. They gazed over the wild country without too exclusive an interest in caribou. The high basin was walled in by three mountain ranges and there was no knowing exactly when or where the caribou traveled outside of their main migrations, and even then their patterns were in flux. In recent years the Nelchina herd had abandoned their normal winter grounds, a sign that they had outstripped their food supply. State biologists feared a population crash like the one that decimated the herd twenty-five years ago and they had called on Alaska hunters to thin the herd.

They angled to the right, hiking among willows, dwarf birch, blueberries and caribou lichen. When they were three hundred feet higher in altitude than the lake, they stopped and made camp on the level fold of a ridge spiked with ten foot spruce trees.

"Eureka," she said.

"It's a good place to glass from."

The rainfly whipped up and down in the wind like their own private banner until they had drawn it down tight on the dome of the tent and hooked it in place. He was pushing the tent stakes into the moss when he noticed her heading down the hill again, a daypack on her shoulder. "Where to?"

She held up an empty canteen. "We forgot the water."

"I'll come with you."

"You don't have to."

"I know I don't have to."

She had seen the bear tracks in the mud by the lake as clearly as he, and didn't object when he reached his rifle out of the tent and followed her down to the water's edge.

Paxson Lake is long and fairly narrow. As they descended, their view toward either end of the lake, left and right, was curtailed by the low-hanging cloud. Opposite, the mountains loomed fleetingly. The water in the lake was bluish gray, chilling to look at. The evening was a sunless shifting of gray shades, but the slope underfoot was green, rich, and vibrant with an archaic purity.

The larger waves had lain down but the lake surface swirled in the gusts, roughened by the uneven bombardments of rain. A thick mist ribboned the far shores of the lake. Everything thrummed. Nothing bespoke anything but what the ages had always known.

"How's it going?" he asked her.

She squatted in the mud pumping the lake water through the ceramic of a pocket water filter.

"Slowly but surely."

"Too many gadgets and it won't be a poor man's hunt anymore. What'll we do for kicks?"

"You won't let me forget I said that."

He shrugged, looking across the lake. "That battery was charged to thirteen and a half volts. I figured it would last six hours. It lasted a hundred minutes."

"Those motors are rated in water tanks, you know that." A second quart bottle was full and she held a third under the filter outlet.

"My turn," he said.

"No, I'm all right."

"Hey," he said.

"What?"

"What the hell. Look at that," he whispered. He dropped to a squat beside her, staring across the lake. "Christ, I thought it was ducks, or geese."

"What is it?"

"Antlers."

Out of the obscurity of fog the heads of eight caribou took shape on the water. They drew near, oblivious of the man and woman squatting on the shore. They swam with their heads high, their wide hoofs paddling under the water. Their crossing was silent and swift.

"Sit down," he said.

"Why?"

"Be still."

She watched him raise the rifle. "It's not even nine o'clock," she said.

"I know that." He wedged his right knee down in the mud and popped the rifle's scope covers. The legal game was cows or bulls of six points or less.

"Are they good?" she asked.

"They're good."

The caribou made shore fifty feet upwind of them. One after another they stepped up on the land and shook the water from their coats. A calf swimming in the rear was the last to clamber up.

"The cow in the middle," he said. "Watch her."

The cow was a fine one, easily over two hundred pounds, white-rumped, her neck mane dripping water. Her antlers, heavy ones, swept back and upwards. A wreath of mist rose from her back.

"She's beautiful," she said. "Go on, shoot her if you want, I don't mind."

He ticked off the safety and she winced in anticipation of a shot. The caribou milled for a few seconds, and with no lazy ado they were on the move again. They had no idea of the threat to them. Their grace was natural, their silence without stealth.

The south wind blew through the mountains, through the glacial passes and across the lake, propelling the clouds, flowing around the finite forms of man and woman, boulder and filigreed moss, dwarf birch and banded caribou. The moment extended beyond its outward duration with an intensity it was impossible to sustain. He held the cow in the crook of his finger for a second longer, her neck transfixed in the crosshairs of his scope, and then he raised his face and watched her without the optics. She fell in with the other caribou and the eight of them mounted their trail and got on with their perennial journey.

"Why didn't you do it?" she said.

He reengaged the safety. "It didn't feel right."

"You'd be justified. It's only three hours."

"I know it." He was hungry again, searching the terrain ahead. He would use the first ring of spruce trees for cover—circle to the south and intercept them.

"You've put plenty into this hunt," she said. "It's fair enough. It's even."

He watched the brown calf trailing and then it too was gone among the trees.

"No, it's not even," he said. "It hasn't been even for ten thousand years. Let's get out of here."

Up the hill they were relieved to get out of the rain and to change their wet things for dry sweats. It was a large tent and they could stand and move around in it. She brushed out her hair and became frisky and talkative, the more so as he was abstracted if not glum. The heat put out by their one-burner stove was substantial and by the end of their meal they had taken their wool hats off and were snug inside and out. They spread out their double sleeping bag and opened the brandy.

"If we'd come a little later we would never have seen them," he said.

"Strange. As if they were never there."

"We'd see their footprints."

"Yes, but footprints don't last."

"No, they don't."

"It was exciting," she said. "I didn't know if it was your heart or mine beating. You won't be disappointed if we don't see another?"

"I might."

"Don't feel bad."

"I'm not."

"You are, I can tell."

He had a sense that he had been offered a gift and turned it down for unclear reasons. He was sullen because of that, he had a vague shame about it. How much shame he would have felt if he had shot the caribou three hours before it was legal, he wasn't sure. There was an irony in his not shooting the caribou when so many of them were said to be doomed anyway.

"Why didn't I do it?"

"Because she was female, because she was beautiful, because she was illegal."

"You wanted me to do it."

"No, I thought you might do it, but I didn't want you to."

"It sounded like you did."

"I wanted you to be pleased with the trip."

"The chances of getting caught are zilch. I believe I was justified. But still, it felt wrong. So much was going through my head. The broken oar. The cheap motor. The Fish & Wildlife cop who tried to bust me for shooting grouse because he was staking out a bull moose for himself and wanted it quiet. The guy that rammed me with his boat because I was hunting pintails and he didn't like it, remember that? I'm chest deep in water and he's up there burning gas in twin outboards. Smiling fraud. I should've put one right in his hull."

"You were thinking these things?"

"It all flashed through my head. They want us to harvest fifteen thousand caribou in two years to save the herd—I should have felt good about taking her."

"Why didn't you?"

"Because it has nothing to do with these fine people, that's why. I didn't want to feel angry when I took her. It's between me and the caribou, not me and anyone else."

"You and the caribou."

"Yes, don't be snide. Me and the caribou and you."

"And me?"

"You. Me and you and the time before I ever killed anything."

"I don't understand."

"You, did you really want me to do it?"

"No, I told you I didn't want you to do it. I didn't want you to be disappointed. How often do we get a sitter anymore and take trips like this?"

"You're right." He licked the brandy off his lips, watching her. "You know, when you said I should do it—"

"I never said you should do it."

"Something in your voice, when you said it, it sounded just like you sounded the first time you said I should go ahead and come inside you if I wanted."

"What?" She drew back in surprise, her breath escaping in an odd laugh. "All this was in your head?"

"Funnily enough, yes."

In her jade-green shift, clutching his shoulders and looking up at him. *Do, if you want, I don't mind, I'd like it.* It was hard to say who if either of them had gotten the better of it.

"Twelve years," he said.

"Terrible ones, I hope."

In answer he joined his mouth to hers and brought her down on the tent floor.

"Give me a minute." She rose and unzipped the tent door.

While she was outside he stuffed their trash into a gallon bag and brightened the lantern by jacking the fuel pump. Then he sat and toyed with the GPS set, bending his head over the device and working the keypad with his fingers. It was August 9, 1996.

On returning and seeing him busy with it, she slipped out of her sweats and took a French bath while the rain pattered on the tent roof.

"Will you keep it?" she asked.

He looked over at her. She was kneeling in a corner of the tent washing herself with water from a canteen. Her face was towards him.

"I don't know," he said.

"If it's too good for you I'll return it."

He considered her remark, weighing the GPS in his hand. "This thing changes everything," he said.

"You're in one of your Luddite moods."

"No."

"Buried treasure's no fun anymore." She mocked him. "Throw your compass away while you're at it. Throw your rifle away. I'll do without birth control, you do without sex."

"Hurry up, you'll catch cold," he said.

She pulled on her sweats and came over to him.

"It's just a big house of cards anyway," he said. "A big fake Jerusalem of words, justifications, hype, technologies. I've got no problem with this, it just never gets us any closer to anything but our limits, whatever out there's beyond us. Of course I'll keep it."

They drew the sleeping bag around them then and made love. The fire in the lantern wavered and dimmed and they replaced it with the light of a pearl-colored candle. The candlelight tussled with their shadows and through the sheer stuff of the tent cast a flickering glow outside on the moss, visible in every direction, a momentary beacon over the lake.

There was a whisper, a laugh, then the radiance vanished and their site on the hill was dark. The windward side of the dome tent contracted and buckled. The rain fell steadily on the tent. It fell steadily on the mosses and lichens, the shrubs and spry trees.

They didn't see another caribou that trip. In the morning he glassed the lake country, but the visibility was poor, the lenses had to be constantly dried, and, disoriented, he put the binoculars away and watched the fog thicken.

But they did find fresh caribou droppings in the moss around the tent. A band of caribou had wandered through their camp in the night. "How do you like that," she said. She was tired of the foul weather and wanted to cut the trip short.

As the lake was calm and the breeze ran in their favor, he agreed. With no power on the boat, and with one oar bent crooked, he expected a long row back to their put-in spot.

Soon their tent was taken down and their backpacks leaned together in the moss.

"Like we were never even here," she said, smiling at him.

He drew in his breath, gazing over Paxson Lake and the surrounding foothills. He stood on the soft green place where their tent had been and, moved by a thought, he extended the GPS receiver in his palm. It was a modest device for one that mediated the secrets of heaven and earth. Another satellite spun into range, time and distance were swiftly reckoned.

"North 62 degrees, 51 minutes, 6.78 seconds," he read the coordinates to her. "West 145 degrees, 35 minutes, 25.68 seconds. Like we were never even here," he said.

And with that he put the device away and reached for her hand.

Brief Stop on the Flyway

The scones were done and Bonnie Hillrunner was sliding them out of the oven when a racket of gunshots sounded from the fields and sloughs beyond the house. In her hand the glass baking pan asserted its weight unexpectedly and—"damn!"—she dropped it with a shudder on the stovetop.

Eastward in the sky a flock of geese went winging over the berms and yellowing wood lots toward the Tanana River. She had forgotten there would be shooting today. A smile labored on her mouth as she drew the oven mitt from her hand, gazing out the dusty window. Every day you had to wake up and face it again.

A small sedan was approaching on the long dirt farm lane. "Doris," she said. And even spoken aloud, the word was incredible to her. How many years was it?

Bonnie went and examined herself in the full-length mirror in the hallway. She raised her chin, spun around, turned sideways and spurred herself with a slap to the thigh. "Tally ho, baby," she said.

Doris—Alston was the name of her late second husband; her second *late* husband—leaned stiffly to the right, considering her face in the rear-view mirror. Lines bracketed her mouth; another, a deep groove plunged vertically between her eyes. No artifice of expression softened the hard set of her features. She drew her hand across her brow, along the hairline, and sat back with a sigh, refocusing on the dirt lane ahead. Frank, Frank, she thought. He could boast two widows now. Two at a time, just like he always wanted. We're all two-timers now, she thought.

Something hit under the axle—a rock maybe. She eased up on the pedal, scanning in the mirror for rubble behind her. Treetops, sky. A trio of sandhill cranes, tall brown creatures with feathery duffs, lolled in the field to her left. Shaggy green pastures gave way to muddy potato lots and hayfields on both sides of the road.

She was suddenly aware of the log farmhouse ahead and the sight filled her with wonder. My God, she thought. The rough-and-ready picturesqueness of her life here, the making shift at every turn—it all came back to her, and she gazed back through memories so vivid she could smell the absent plumbing, squeeze up the mittfuls of bluegrass seed, and fumble through the midwinter nights in unelectrified darkness.

A woman strode out of the farmhouse to meet her. Flowing white skirt, full sweater, both hands resting on her forward hip—Bonnie, unmistakably.

"When I left Delta," Doris heard herself saying a minute later, when she had emerged from the rented car and looked south over the fields to Mount Hayes and the snow peaks of the Alaska Range, "I thought I was leaving for good. This was my favorite view."

"It is such a kick in the pants to see you, Doris."

"Then I've done what I came to do. I'll go home."

A husky laugh from Bonnie. "Don't you do that to me."

The cold September morning was cut early from winter like the first wedge of a round of cheese. Splashes of yellow brightened the country from the waste willows to the highest lovely birches. Windrows of mown hay lay steaming in the fields. A red tractor ground along towing a machine which Doris in her fever of nostalgia recognized as "the old baler!" its tumbler still turning, sheaving up the cut piles and leaving behind the neat wan blocks of pressed brome.

"Who's haying for you?"

"Friend of Frank's. I'm running late with oats and barley. I'm going to have to hire some men. Come in, Doris."

"I came as soon as I could."

"There just wasn't time. You know how we feel about embalming. We had twenty-four hours to bury him."

"If you'd let me know he was ill." Doris preceded her into the familiar living room.

"The man was in excellent health until two months ago."

"I might have done something. You say his liver—? I don't remember Frank having a problem."

Gunshots crackled at a remove from the house but the women were too intent on their meeting to pay it any mind.

"You mean liquor? He never touched the stuff. No, a world traveler's been called home," Bonnie said in an elevated tone of voice which, together with the arching of her eyebrows, infused her words with too mysterious a meaning for Doris to take any comfort in them.

"Will you tell me what you're talking about?"

"His Africa days—his malaria."

"What about it?"

"The quinine treatments. It scarred his liver. All these years the scars were hardening inside him. Nobody knew it. Harder and harder, till the blood vessels burst."

"Oh, dear." Doris, fourteen years a practicing nurse in Sacramento, sat on the edge of an armchair sorting this information in her mind while Bonnie paced the florid rug in front of her, obviously braless under her oversize knit sweater.

"He vomited blood. Liver pushed the blood up his stomach wall. His esophagus ballooned with it." Bonnie's account was interrupted by the single report of a gunshot outside. Both women looked toward the window.

"What is that shooting?" Doris said.

"Hunters, I suppose."

"On your land?"

"If we can hear it, it's our land. Didn't Frank always say that? Anyway, they cleaned the blood out and he came home. Ordered ten yards of sludge for a new pasture and got a crazy idea of roofing the house again."

Doris smiled, laying her head back and contemplating the ridgebeam twenty feet above her, a massive lacquered log of white spruce.

Bonnie went on: "He woke spitting blood at five one morning. We had a wild ride to the hospital. They couldn't stop it." She spoke in passionate but measured accents as if she were telling a hard story to a child whom she wished to reassure not frighten. It was the tone in which she spoke of the madness of governments and the world's redemptive slide toward its end. "What's the matter with me? I've got scones and spiced tea. Give me a second."

While Bonnie was occupied in the kitchen, Doris left her chair and wandered through the living room. She found the obituary on the rolltop desk by the picture window, a newspaper clipping which she hesitated over and finally picked up in her hand. She stared at the black-and-white photograph, a grainy likeness of Frank Hillrunner considerably aged since she had known him, and after twice reading the accompanying six-paragraph biography, she lowered the clipping to the desk and gazed out the window at the range of snow peaks rising in the blue September sky twenty-five miles away.

Those mountains, so close and so immense, used to affect her with a kind of breathlessness, a rapture of her senses not unlike what happened to her when a man loomed above her in the act of love, only here there was no passing vigor, no flagging warmth, no change at all except as eons go. She remembered one morning being out with Frank and the children when the clouds sped over the whitened peaks causing them to seem to teeter toward her in an illusion so powerful as to fill her with dread, with a foretaste of catastrophe.

Frank Hillrunner. Friends called him Haystack. Fought in the Pacific. One of the biggest haying operations in the state. Sometime civic leader. Active in his fellowship. Survived by wife Bonita and eight children. Eight children by three women none of whom was Bonnie, Doris noted.

Behind her in the open kitchen there were sounds of sliding drawers and chinking silver. Doris didn't turn from the window but asked, "Did he have much pain?"

"What?"

"Pain."

"No, he had no pain," Bonnie said. "None he complained of. You know Frank. Worst pain was he couldn't work. No energy."

She entered carrying a tray on which two mugs of hot clove-smelling tea flanked a heap of scones oozing raspberry jam. There was a knock at the door just then and Bonnie, her eyes searching the room in protest, halted with the tray in her hands, at a loss how to react.

"Here, let me," Doris said. And Doris, always quick to actions of mercy, in a flash had lifted the service from Bonnie's hands.

Bonnie composed herself and answered the door. The caller was a hunter, a local man. She recognized his bearded, high-boned face but she couldn't quite place him. A worn camouflage jacket rode his shoulders, a duckcloth cap covered his head, and a wooden goose call hung from a line around his neck.

"Mrs. Hillrunner," he said.

Two companions waited below in the yard. A net bag stuffed with goose decoys projected over the back rail of their pickup truck. Doris drew nearer trying to hear the man's words and he noticed her and touched the bill of his cap in greeting, a gesture which she hadn't seen in ages, not since before she moved to California.

"I'm sorry," Bonnie replied, "but he isn't here. Frank passed away last weekend."

The news was received by the caller with pitiful and undisguised dismay. Bonnie, to save him the embarrassment, stepped outside with him, and their conversation continued outside, audible to Doris as a give and take of murmurs.

Alone, Doris drifted back through the living room, squaring its corners with those of her memory. She stopped at the window and looked out at them, the three hunters gathered around Bonnie in attitudes of meek condolence, their heads bowed as they listened to her, her lips moving and her arm commandingly outstretched, the raglan sleeve swaying as she pointed across the fields at whatnot. Bonnie's silver ponytail swept her shoulders, bound by a colored elastic whose purpose, it seemed to Doris, was not to constrain the hair but to be available at whatever vital moment Bonnie chose to pluck it out and shake her hair free. Doris, watching through the transparent shade of her own reflection, was conscious of her own spartan hair, dyed brown and tucked at the edges—certified, registered hair. Truly, Frank had found a suppler woman in Bonnie, one who milked the world of the good things it offered and even in age was comfortable to tread the mud where dreams root. Better for Doris, less painful, if Bonnie had simply been younger.

"What did they want?"

Bonnie fell back in the sofa, twisting her fingers over her knees. "People tell me I'm strong, but that's on the outside. I've never been so agitated, Doris. I need to get away. I may sell the place."

"Don't be hasty about it."

"I'm surrounded by junk mail. Who expected it?"

"It's a blessing, Bonnie. My Dale took three years."

"It must have been hell for you."

"I kept a journal. I read it afterwards. Felt less guilty then. You see, I finally put him in a home because I couldn't take another day of it." Doris licked the stray jam off her fingers. "Your raspberries?"

A loud boom rattled the windowpanes.

"What in blazes!" Doris rose from her chair. The gunshot was followed by a spate of lesser reports from a farther location. "Would you mind telling me—?"

"It's the geese and cranes flying through, Doris. Frank's friends were always welcome to hunt the property. Standing invitations."

"Why don't you stop them?"

"Don't have the heart I guess."

"The heart!"

"Don't even know where their blinds are."

"And those three?"

"I told them to hunt if they wanted."

"You didn't."

Bonnie nodded, sipping her tea. "I wish you'd been here, Doris. We washed him in rose oil and wrapped him in white silk. Friends dug the hole and built the coffin."

"Is he here?"

"Back of the house."

"Of course he is." Doris settled back in her chair, looking toward the window, the daylight outside. "It's a different world here."

"It was a beautiful event."

"What kind of day was it, Bonnie?"

"Well, it rained, a little. Didn't bother anyone. The man was so loved. There were shovels for all to pitch in. It was beautiful to see."

They pursued their memories in silence.

"He had his fill of the world," Doris reflected.

"That he did. He kept an open mind, he did for his brother and sister. That's what killed him. Malaria for God's sake! It's not enough they tried to shoot him for leading a rebel brigade."

Doris remembered the Uganda story and laughed.

"He gave us many wonderful years," Bonnie said.

"Some of the years were wonderful," Doris agreed. "Some weren't so hot."

There was another rattle of gunfire outside, twelve-bores blasting somewhere on the farm, the echoes spreading over two thousand acres of tilled earth and wildwood and marsh.

"How can you stand it!" The final shot brought Doris to her feet. Her nerves were unstrung, her knuckles all protruding.

"I don't think Frank would have minded."

"It's not fireworks, Bonnie, they're not saluting him, they're taking advantage of you. You've just put him in the ground!"

"Frank had some awful war memories, but shooting never bothered him. Do you know what the scariest sound he ever heard in his life was?"

Doris exhaled irritably, pacing the room.

"It was the sound of icebergs cracking up," Bonnie said, "up in Labrador when he worked there, a banshee cry that chilled him to the soul. And the second scariest sound? Your voice, Doris, your Wisconsin accent when you flew off the handle at him."

Doris had come to the window and she didn't turn from it, but gazed at the sky, its jagged blue beginnings in the mountains, the roots of heaven reaching down. When she stirred, squinting through the glass, her breath blown softly back at her, she said, "So he traded in my accent for a Montana show girl."

"That's right." Bonnie nodded, in spite of herself. Watching Doris, noticing the bony contours of her head and back and shoulders framed in the brighter window, she reminded herself that the competition was long since over and won.

"That's about the size of it, Doris. Fair is fair. Now I'll get more tea." And rocking forward on her feet, standing from the sofa, Bonnie was overcome by a moment's faintness, her blood shifting within. She balanced until it passed, sighing over a thousand little regrets but none of them mortal, her sweater lifting and settling on the long bulbs of her breasts which had nourished three infants in their time and outlasted all of the men who had pressed and sweated against them.

"Now there's a big flock. I can hear them honking," Doris called.

Bonnie hastened back from the kitchen with a steaming mug of tea in each hand. She left them on the coffee table and joined Doris at the window. Sixty or seventy birds flying in a liquid V were fast approaching from the northwest. "We get mostly white-fronteds and Canadas," she said. "That looks like Canadas."

Their long black necks stretching downward in unison, the birds wheeled around an invisible pivot. On every head a white blaze flashed: something small became something vast. Their wings beat up and down with languid grace.

"It's beautiful," Doris let her breath out.

"They're in for a look-see," Bonnie said. "Look, they're setting their wings, they're going to land."

The honking was spirited and became even louder. The birds swept in with their leaders but the shapeliness of the flock deteriorated. The geese at the flock's periphery suddenly flared out and the flock slowed in weird confusion. Bonnie and Doris both started at the window. Shots were being fired from nearby pit blinds or ground thickets. There were several blasts and three, four birds folded and fell. It wasn't over yet. The geese were stupid with fear and sixty yards in the air didn't put them out of range. Another hunting party waited to the east. A flurry of shots, a pair of Canadas went down.

Doris was shaking with emotion when she turned to Bonnie. "How many are out there?"

"Frank had lots of friends."

"You keep saying that."

"Six-eight hunting parties?"

"How can you let them!"

"Let them?" In distraction Bonnie returned to the sofa and sat down. "I've had plenty of worries, Doris." She grasped her mug too vehemently and the tea scalded her fingers. Odd how Frank's death was written in Africa decades before she even knew him. Malaria! The odd fact stuck in Bonnie's mind. Everything appeared insubstantial in light of it. Its craziness was somehow consonant with the way she had lived her life—with a certain cavalierness she would never go so far as to regret. She glanced at Doris who didn't seem to be struck by this element of silliness in Frank's death. "What exactly are you objecting to?"

"It hurts me to see it—today of all days."

"Frank never stood on ceremony."

"Those geese haven't got a chance, Bonnie." Doris tore herself away from the window. "Don't forget, I'm living down the flyway now. I've seen what's happened to their wetlands. It's a terrible shame. Those creatures are greater travelers than you or I or Frank could ever be."

"Don't get high and mighty with me, Doris. We nest geese here every spring, we're good hosts to them. I was never careless of another living thing."

"I know that, Bonnie, I'm sorry." Doris hastened into her chair and leaned across the armrest toward her. "They're life mates, don't you see? Family birds."

"I understand. Heartbreak might be too strong a word for it, but—hurt, consternation, who's to say the geese aren't capable of it?"

"You do understand."

"I do. They aren't china birds."

Doris turned her face a few degrees. "What aren't you saying?"

"Nothing. Only you're lying to yourself if you think they're cut from a special cloth."

"Lying?"

"Life mates, maybe, but it's not as though they wait for death or divorce."

"What nonsense."

"Bite and snap and honk and you can't tell me the ganders aren't looking under their wings at all the gooses because I see it happen every spring. It's a peep show."

"Fiddlesticks! How can you say that to me?"

"There's always plenty under the surface, Doris."

"You think I don't know that?" Doris flung out of her chair and seized the obituary off the rolltop desk.

"I didn't write that," Bonnie said.

"I ought to crumple this in my hand, but I can't do it," Doris said. She let the paper fall to the desktop. "Decorated seaman. Delta pioneer. Missionary.

Farmer. Mayor. Innovator. Philanderer. Adulterer. Oh it's all there."

"He was a good man, Doris."

"He was *not* a good man." Doris stamped her foot and lowered her voice, swinging down into her chair. "Or I don't know what is. Can you be a good man and not a good father? God knows I loved him, Bonnie, but nobody can say that man was a good father to his children."

"He changed, Doris. Young people hereabouts, they adopted him, they called him dad."

"Rubbish! Old men are frauds and you know it."

There was more shooting outside.

"Again!"

Both women jumped to their feet.

"Doris—"

Doris had started toward the window; she balked and raised her hands to her face. She was crying.

"Help me get lunch," Bonnie said.

"I'm not staying."

"Can't you?"

Doris was already looking for her purse.

"You've come all this way," Bonnie pleaded with her.

"I had to come." Doris drew the purse strap over her shoulder and looked Bonnie full in the face. "You'll have your hands full, it sounds like. Boarding horses this winter?"

"Turning them down. Had a bear kill a foal in July."

They were moving toward the door as they talked.

"I'm sorry to hear that."

"You, Doris?"

"Oh, I'm always needed at the hospital. I won't retire for another two years."

"Not if you can help it, right?"

"That's right." Doris smiled and they stopped in the doorway. Bonnie slid her hand up the edge of the open door and propped her other hand on her hip.

"You won't stay?"

"I can't."

"I believe Frank never stopped loving you, Doris. Please take that thought with you."

"Thank you for saying that."

"Oh and—" Bonnie hurried back to the coffee table and brought three scones wrapped in a white cloth. "To feed the ducks," she said.

Doris tucked the bundle into her purse without comment.

The sun was high and the day much warmer now. Doris gazed once more at the majestic mountains, deep blue in their bastions, the snowy cones struck off across the sky. East, the waters of the Clearwater and the Tanana and the Goodpaster Rivers were gathering, and in the west over the hayfields the yellowing flags of the hardwood trees marked the public road and the town of Delta Junction and the Delta River flowing north beyond them.

"It's not far from heaven, anyway," Doris said.

They crossed the yard together, the two old rivals, side by side to the front east corner of the house, where Bonnie stopped and watched Doris go on alone.

"He's due north a hundred feet, you can't miss him," Bonnie said. "Feet toward the mountains like he wanted."

"I'll be leaving directly from there," Doris called.

"I understand."

The wild grasses rustled as she parted them, picking her way toward the grave. The frost would blast the rose hips soon. The iris heads were sere and brown.

Old Blue at Sundown

Drank my last cup of coffee sixty-three years ago: ten o'clock in the night we were driving a dray team delivering coal from a wagon and folks had us in for cakes and coffee, it was good coffee too: 1936: a hard winter in Sioux Falls, below zero and the coal being rationed. They taught us in school there's nothing worse for your stomach than coffee with cream curdled in it. Grownups waking in the morning to bitter coffee and toast burnt on a cookstove stoked with corncobs. Sixty-three years ago I drank my last cup of coffee and I wish I had another.

The massive log of hemlock jutting out of the truck bed above him seemed to uphold or defy the grave darkening sky. Between seizures of pain he was almost comfortable. From side to side he rocked, twisting to a sitting position, his struggles recorded and expunged in the bed of sand. With care he guided his fingers down his leg to the left knee and, beyond it, round, immense, yielding in points but immoveable, the truck tire. He ran his palms up its gritty, treaded circumference, searching for leverage, then extended his arms and embraced the tire, clinging to it like a castaway to his float. He lay back and waited.

He had never been in a fix he couldn't fox his way out of one way or another. Somebody was bound to come along. On the now-deserted strand he had seen by day a dozen or more beachgoers. "How are you?" "Oh as good as the weather." From Anchorage they traveled to fish and to clam, clogging the roads to the tip of Homer Spit. What's an octogenarian winching logs off the beach for if it ain't to show off? "A pioneer," they whisper. "What's your secret, mister?" Secret? Well, I eat toast and milk every breakfast of my life, never made myself a slave to any thing, never was a know-it-all, always patronized the poor grocer in town, I loved some women that pushed the time beside me, but I never was a sideman to anyone.

Cold cardboard shells of yesterday's rockets littered the beaches. Lurching again from the waist, he struggled to free himself: shoved at the lugged tire, drummed at the side wall, picked at the flanged nuts, flailed at the wheel well, struck at the truck body with both fists and all his heart invested in an effort no man could win at.

Exhaling, he subsided in the sand, his eyes drawing down and grimacing face turned to the flooding sea. His leg didn't anguish him, or the pain was indistinct from the nauseating weight that pressed on his body and periodically seemed to crack him in half while he squeezed his head in his hands or chewed his spotted knuckles or sang out or even in dizzying, suffocating moments, laughed.

Just hold on, somebody will come. Driving into the sand without the tires or transmission for it. People have no sense. I wonder how many I pulled from hazard in my time—and now it's me and not a soul in earshot. He heard a popping of fireworks down the beach and, scooting sideways, peered down the curving shoreline to the Spit and the lighted beachfront. *July brings out the wild ones, they drink and head for a spin on the beach—they'll be along.*

But you were off your feed to turn the engine off, Lance. With the tide coming in? It was a fool thing to do. Groping forward of the tire, he felt for the slipped jack where it might be expected to have settled in the sand. For an instant his heart leapt when his left-hand fingers clenched an object which, as he brought it near, gleamed dully: a rogue lump of coal. Not to despair, he extended the coal in his right hand, writhing and twisting in an effort to reach with it the fallen flashlight. Oh, the shame of it. Grain by grain the flashlight was sinking. Quartz particles flashed in the funnel of sand at its head.

The faces of his wives brooded over him, radiating terse amusement as an intricate system of plugs, pipes, wires and cylinders opened forth in his brain. He found comfort in the solving of mechanical probabilities—perhaps too much comfort. Through the reek of sea air he smelled her oil (Old Blue was bleeding) and guessed he had broken a seal in driving her aground. Diagrams exploded in his skull. He pictured the manifold lying across the battery cable and running down the battery. "I'll bet that's it." He spoke aloud, as if to his retriever

Red. "If the cable insulation was crumbled, the battery was hot, the exhaust pipe grounded..." The simplicity of his error stunned him. Silently the juice had run out of her. She would have idled just fine but didn't have the amperage to be cold-cranked. *You should never have stopped her by the saltwater, Lance.* He lunged at the cone of yellow light: sand splashed the lens, mouse-like shadows flitted past. *Old Blue, she's been a good rig, faithful horse for thirty-one years. I more than once forgot an anniversary but never an oil change. Carla saying I cared more about my machines than about her and the kids. Sally used to say the same thing. A long time ago it was. What's your secret? If I was stuck in my ways, maybe they was lucky ways. Now I'm just a stern old bachelor who doesn't care about anyone but himself.*

A mewing gull circled in the sky, tracing its quavering treble over the water, a sound so high and so thin, it would have seemed, except for its high lonesomeness, not to be mortal at its source. He thought he recognized the song, his gaze widening under the blue vastness of the twilight. Going Across the Sea? Streets of Laredo? Memories echo; echoes haunt memories. Was it as simple as a song? With Spanish strains and graven with bass notes? Or in the end the music lover himself composes his testament on the instruments at hand, hugging that tire in a strange embrace, a string man clinging to his upright bass.

Far down the beach a cluster of firecrackers exploded and Lance heard a muffled bang and another bang bang and it was like the banging on the bangboard of the wagon at picking time in October and November when the husked ears were flipped up and banged on the bangboard before sliding down into the open bag. They had a big-bellied boiler in the back where they saved the best ears for seed corn. Suddenly excruciated, Lance bit down on the chunk of coal, grinding his teeth in it, and convulsed in a great shiver; spat out his black tongue and retched and stretched his arm toward the light. *I feel it, I feel it now.* He groped for the air valve beyond his knee knowing the tire would deflate no further. Holler! Making public his pain was never his way but he could learn. Holler! The flashlight lay beyond him, its cup of light dimming, the grains of sand running down. *I spilt the light. The sweet, sweet light.*

It's got to be all mashed to hell. Give me a knife, I'd jigsaw through the knee bones. It's like a deer, honey. Sooner do without my leg than lie here forever. If I had a knife. A hammer. A mouth harp. Saw it back and forth and blow. Think of all the songs I know. Red River and Wabash Cannonball and Blue Eyes Crying and Will the Circle and When the Saints and Folsom Blues. All those ballads rags reels. Harmonica got its due back then. The early days before bluegrass was Bluegrass. First time I heard Bill Monroe in Chicago it was 1934 and a comet lit the sky, just picked you up and didn't put you down. Balls of fire! They said Bill Monroe was playing his mandolin at a schoolhouse in Nebraska and singing with Charlie his brother so I spent all my money getting there and back, it give me such courage I told Sally I loved her so baldly she asked me was it liquor talking, I said no it's the old-time music I been hearing. "That hillbilly stuff again?"

She liked to rile me. You mark my words, Sally, this man croons and laughs and howls like a wind, his mandolin, I tell you, it's possessed—if he's not on the Opry before Roosevelt's out of office I'll eat my hat and you can marry someone else. Blushes and dimples. I understand now a woman's dimples are like the cornflowers: they have their purpose and their season. Town folks, Sally's was, Sal the family baker smelled a lot like my mother, warm and yeasty, hair light brown, amber tresses fine as any daydreamer could wish for. Won't you ever let your bangs down? "I always let my hair down at night," she says. Now what would it take for me to ever get to see that? Then it finally comes down: the curtain rises on a brand new show. It's an old old show only the figgers and picklers always change, the fickers and piddlers I mean, fiddlers and pickers. It counted for something that every-body roundabouts was talking about yours truly Lance West the young feller that picks a hundred bushels a day and never leaves a white rag on an ear. I hook it, I shuck it, I'd do it tomorrow if I could get back tonight: grasp it and break it and flip it up at the bangboard, such a good solid feeling that was. Worst of the Depression was over, I left Pa and Ma and Kenny on the farm and got a job in town for twenty cents an hour building silos. A good wage and lucky to have it. Boss tells you to run, you run, a gang of hungry men watching from the door. Roosevelt passes a law and the pay goes up to thirty-five cents an hour, I come home that night hollering Made three dollars fifty cents today!

He counted the visible stars, dozens of blue and silver glimmers in the heavens. The ripe smell of the sea wafted towards him, the waves broke gently on the stones and rubbing up and down the beach made washboard sounds. Lance propped up on his elbow, staring at the dark peaked shadow under the truck: silhouette of the bedded rock that broke Old Blue. *It's a damn funny thing how one thing leads to another.* A wave of nausea roared through him and his eyelids flickered. He heard the intermittent slap of a keel in the water and was going to call out to it—a skiff in the bay—had even raised his hand in a gesture of supplication, when his efforts dissolved in not the dark of the moment but a distracting light of memory, a ghost dust stopped his mouth, a rusty bail creased his palm, and his sharp, blue eyes smarted in the fumes of an old oil lamp.

Dust rose in the storms and buried the fences, it got so dark by day you lit a kerosene lamp to eat your dinner by at noon. We stayed through the Dust Bowl. Corncobs was our Lincoln Logs, corncobs our fuel. No wonder I come away when I did. Blacksmith left, store clerk left, banker left too. Folks heading west. Fruit tramps. Little Rose Maddox the Hillbilly Filly from Alabama to California just a child she was, singing in the fruit camps. Listen, Sally, it ain't the badlands, it ain't as bad as that, but we're a dry-farming horse-farming dirt-farming family with a hundred sixty acres some head of cattle scarce hogs chickens field corn oats barley I won't take you back there, I won't, Sal, I won't. Then I seen that ad in the Cheyenne paper in '38 CARPENTERS WANTED IN ALASKA and away I come. Don't let your love die, Sally, I'll be back in a year or two, I promise I will. Was as good as my word, too, only nobody figured on the war.

Lance turned his head suddenly, hearing the water scurry up the beach towards him. Laid his cheek down in the sand and saw the moon hover slowly on the sea. It was only a seiner's harbor light, made soft and scumbled by a mist. The smooth hum of its engines soothed him and he closed his eyes and glided homeward on it. *Midnight on the stormy deep. Sailors out there somewhere. Funny this morning the fog creeping into the bay between the islands. Step out of your house in the morning, you might never step in again. The town ain't much, but this country's the finest I've seen, the wild parsnip and the purple lupine and wild geranium spreading violet shadows under the wild pink rose, the snow-topped mountains across the bay. Would everything be different if I had brought her here instead of Fairbanks? Smack in the heart of big sky country, Fairbanks, and you'd think a Dakota girl would understand a thing like space and cold and homestead lonesomeness only things was changed in a subtle way after the war and Sal was always a city gal at heart. Me building overtime for the contractors, I guess she hauled one bucket of water, one cord of wood too many, what with Robby being born, and by the time I finally sank a well and ran electric, it was already too—* "it's like living on the moon!"—*too late.*

Handy as I am, I couldn't make the moon a pleasant place to live. They always take the kids when they go, and when it happens a second time, it's a nightmare you've already known. Carla left with Jen, and with John not even born yet, and I guess I ain't wept since then. I don't think I can. They're always so quick with their mouths, by the time he scares up the words in his head a man's left gaping at nothing. Sal took Robby and Carla took Jen and John and more than once I more than once I was glad of it. I spent too much time in the shop like she said but I didn't well like all her grousing and me making canoes and heirloom clocks for her family for Christmas and never getting more mercy for it than her asking how many power saws I intended to acquire in my lifetime and me wanting to know what she expected a man to do with his time except make the fine things it pleases him to make and she saying I don't value her like I value my machines and me saying how dare you judge my love for my children in front of my children and she's just plain tired of bluegrass and gospel anyhow and I never liked eating in restaurants either. What was it she said? The problem with solving problems with problem solutions is—the solutions is sometimes no better than the problems. Smart woman, Carla. Big Minnetonkan with Ojibwa blood and some tricks no man ever dreamed of.

His reverie was interrupted by the herald of a wave, the peculiar clap they make when they brazen up the beach and break on shore. *What have I done?* He saw clearly the white water of her tendered extremities before she drew back again in a sibilant rush. The rank smell inflated his nostrils, his nausea racked him, the fishing boat was gone far down the shore. *A light on a boat riding to harbor so slow in a mist you don't know it's moving. How a thing looks through tears, soft and blurred and bittersweet, tarnished like old silver. The rain washes away the chalklines, eyes run with old age, and you step out of your house in the morning with no more sense than a lamb. Soft shining disk like a dime in my palm, a flashlight slowly sinking in the sand. I always liked the look of a dime in my hand. If you had a dime, you were a rich man. A bottom penny shelf, a top nickel shelf: candies, licorice, cigars, snuff. Never had much money but there was always something to eat. I smelled the bread from the barn where I worked. Rainwater in the cistern, Ma so busy, lye soap for the wash, farm breakfast for the men, dinner, canning, churning, children. And the bread! Oh lord that's bread I still miss the likes of, steaming, rough bread with the thick crust you tore off the heel of, butter slabbed on it and melting, yellow butter dripping down your chin, dizzy with goodness. Oh lord there's nothing like it.*

What have I done? Balancing on the tail of his backbone, his abdominal muscles burning, his left hand gripping his caught leg, right hand feeling along Old Blue's flank, five blind quivering fingers straining higher and farther: nothing: nothing in reach, nothing detachable, nothing to double as a prybar.

He fell back with a gasp, a retch, a rebel's yell. The stars proliferated. The hemlock beam lorded over him, a huge chastisement. *I come looking for spruce or red fir washed up from British Columbia and I seen this hemlock too good to pass up. Fine giant timber I couldn't get my arms around. Ten foot length good for milling. Rafter my new shop with it. Boys come running to watch me lift it, young men and women holding hands. Oh they think you're a character, Lance West, you play the part more than you ought, eighty-three-year-old sourdough with a boom winch welded on his truck, spritely limber old coot. You gonna pick up that log, mister? You watch me.*

With his chainsaw he cut off the punky end of it for firewood—that's money in the bank, you never know when there's gonna be lean times. He looped a chain around an end of the log, drew up the links with a hook, then swung the boom around from the truck and under power winched the log up vertical till it swayed kind of precarious on end, then girdled the lower part of the log with a second chain which he hooked by cable to a comealong anchored to an eye welded on the forward rail of the truck bed. By turns cranking the comealong and powering the boom winch, the truck idling the while, he manipulated the massive log while restraining its side-to-side motion, and by judiciously reversing the truck when he had the purchase of a few inches under the log, and prying with the prybar when the log caught on a rail or corner, he was able to the amazement of the onlookers to hoist the giant hemlock into the truck where it lay all catawampus, jutting into the air but held in tension by the cables reefed tight as he could winch them.

With the log secure, and plenty of wild coal in sight, he stopped to harvest it off the beaches. There was a windfall of coal to be gathered and he little heeded the passing minutes as the seashore emptied of day-trippers. Coal seams in the bluffs, barnacled piles of it, ancient stranded shelves the waves uncovered. He heated his workshops with coal, it was inferior stuff, burned ashy and smoky, but gave heat, and you never know when there's gonna be lean times. He didn't suppose he would ever outgrow the Depression.

The sun westered, and the tide turned. The gulls quieted, congregating in the sand. A cool damp breeze alerted Lance to the lateness of the hour and, straightening, he saw around him a world changed to twilight. The light graded from the fire hues of sundown to the olive purples of the sea. In the drawn-out dusk of deep summer he wished to soak in a tub of hot water, to sit with a bowl of greenhouse strawberries and listen to Jimmie Rodgers or Big Bill Monroe or Roy Acuff. He heaved a last hunk of lignite into Old Blue's bed and, lightly panting, hung his wrists over the rail, wondering that the weight on him of fourscore years should be so slight in comparison. Where does it go? What mechanism compresses, what alembic distills it? What form, if any, does it keep? For years he had gleaned coal and driftwood off the beaches of Homer, Ninilchik, Deep Creek and Whiskey Gulch—took it home to the saws and furnaces that altered it physically, chemically, released its shape and energy. The body likewise has a destiny, a terrible terrestrial destiny. But to the rest of him, to everything else that was in him or of him, the times he lived through, or the times that lived through him, the drive of his life and its untold improvisations, the sweetness of worldly fellowship, the unpossessed spirit of it all—what happens to it?

The breeze ruffled the patient gulls and puffed out their breast feathers. On Homer Spit the lights were coming on. Lance raised and dropped his palms on the vibrating rail. For a moment longer his vague questionings held him. Old Blue was full up. With four-wheel drive, manual transmission, and oversize tires, he never worried about her bogging down in the sand. But now, having taken his place at the wheel, doubtful after all that she would clear at a turn the mansize block of driftwood dead ahead of her, he put her in reverse, and in his haste in the twilight he backed over the rock.

The hemlock log, flung with sudden force against its bands, stove in the cab's rear window, shattering the glass. They grounded on the rock with a harsh wrenching sound. The truck rocked and shuddered. Lance killed the engine and jumped out. He knelt in the sand looking underneath her: the muffler had torn loose and brought the exhaust and tailpipe down with it. The rock bit hard into her belly; he couldn't chip it down with the prybar. He lunged ineffectually at the rock. He dug around but couldn't budge it.

The truck's inclination caused the hemlock log to strain backward against its cables. Lance repositioned the log using the comealong and prybar. He raised the fallen tailpipe off the sand and lashed it to the base of the ball hitch using a twist of wire scrounged from the glass-strewn floor of the cab. On his way forward he tested the log again. There was still too much slack in the cable of the boom winch; he would reel it in under power. When he finally took his place in the seat of the cab, it was with the same certainty with which he had always taken it. He turned the key in the starter, but it didn't start her. He tried it again, but the engine didn't spark. Toeing the pedals, Lance turned the key. Then he jumped out of the truck and faced the sea. He ordinarily never would have killed the engine, not on a beach at flood tide. He reached in and tried the key again. The battery was dead.

"Old Blue," he said.

He raised the hood and checked the contacts at the battery posts. Got the flashlight, checked the contacts, tried the key again. He tramped the beach in dismay. A wave of shell chips, pumice pebbles and sea bladders undulated underfoot, the last high tide line stretching down the beach in both directions. It was clamming tides lately and the night's high would be much higher.

The beach was desolate. Lance started across it on foot. The hike to the paved road would take him an hour. Help would be long in coming. He stopped and looked back at Old Blue. Inches made the difference. If the saltwater got in her engine, she was done for.

With the sea rising, the sky darkening, he hurried to devise a means to move her. He disengaged the clutch of the winch mounted on Old Blue's prow and walked the cable up the beach and dropped its end in the sand, then detached the comealong from the back of the truck and carried it up the beach another forty feet past the first cable end to a boulder where the rusty remnant of an old running line, a metal ring, was bolted. Here he hooked the comealong, then drew its cable truckwards down the beach and softly cursed when its length was payed out and the hooked ends of the two cables lay five feet apart in the sand. He closed the gap with a round of chain unwound from the hemlock log, then stepped back and frowned at the rigging.

Load capacities can't be trusted. He tried it anyhow: high on the beach, he cranked the comealong lever and the cable wobbled and rose to the horizontal. His back ached from all the day's stooping and lifting and winching; what mattered now was saving Old Blue. He ratcheted in the cable and it straightened and tautened. He looked back at the truck. He cranked and cranked, and the cable tightened and tightened to a rigid fastness, but without any forward movement of its load or the sense of easing that precedes it. Eventually, feeling the first ping of slippage in the cable, he dropped the comealong.

He left it hang there at high tension and ran to check for hitches in the rigging. The truck was in neutral. The pawls were in place on the winches. Lance got down and shone the flashlight on the truck's undercarriage. He had been wrong about the truck's not moving: the rock had etched a foot's resistance in Old Blue's belly before adamantly burying its point in her.

He found the tire jack under the passenger seat. In his haste he dropped the flashlight in the sand and had to kneel and grope for it. On straightening, he was startled to see how very dark the evening was. Odd shapes of driftwood started to his awareness. The water was calm but there was an eerie boldness in the lilt of its advance on the land.

Given the rock's position, just ahead of the rear axle, and the angle necessary for the axle to clear the sharp crest of the rock, he stood the jack under the truck's rear left leaf spring where, levered upwards, it duly expanded, raising the truck with it. Awful creaks and violent shudders were the hemlock log's response to the disequilibrium. Lance West was nothing if not a respecter of the material laws of cause and effect: you didn't have to be a superstitious man to balk at finding yourself kneeling in the kill zone of a ten-foot widowmaker. He glanced at its girth above him. In removing one of the log's restraining cables, he hadn't considered that a single cable wouldn't suffice to stabilize the log once the truck was again impelled in even so slight a motion as the winch or jack would impart to it.

He let go of the jack and trained the beam of light under the elevated chassis. Old Blue was on the cusp of clearing the rock. The midges that love a damp shoreline soared around his face. The sense that he had forgotten something, some small but essential detail, troubled him. He stood and stared at the log in the truck bed. The log was of no consequence to him now—he would as soon have jettisoned it. There was a muffled report in the sky over Homer, a bright efflorescence over the town, then fiery sparkles sank through the blue evening and one by one to the last were extinguished. In a festive gesture Lance patted Old Blue's flank and she sprang forward with a sem-blance of eagerness. Through whatever precision of circumstances—the pressure of his hand on the truck, or some tiny act of erosion under the chassis, the rock's resistance to the truck suddenly gave way, and the cable in front being still under high tension, the truck lurched forward. In turn the log recoiling along the rail slammed into Lance and knocked him off his feet. An instant later the truck rolled back and settled on his leg, crushing it below the knee.

He pried, he pulled, he pushed, he prayed: everything he tried availed him nothing. *All that light in a bowl of sand. What a pity. Coal without fire. Dad, you've got to get a cellular phone. How many times they said to me. If you fall and break your hip. If you have a heart attack. Got to think ahead. Oh, I don't mind change, but I don't like surprises. Rockabilly and honky-tonk come along, but it was bluegrass saved the banjo.*

Hello? I've been gathering coal and wood on the beach and I. The old farm phones, the neighbors eavesdropping. There's always something new to crow about. Nowadays they grow stuff their fathers never did. Soybeans. If it ain't new, it don't make money. Pa quit cutting wood and bought a new gas stove with the two hundred dollars I sent him in one-dollar bills in a walnut box with a gold padlock: the money popped out accordion style. Bought them a TV too. The new country music I can't stand—all pop, slick and flashy, I don't understand it.

I'm just a stern old bachelor I guess. Who to call? Sally's gone and Carla's gone deaf. Tap on the phone. Listen, Carla, you were right. About everything. Hello, Jen, may I talk to the little ones? Like milk and daisies, innocent as sunshine. Call Margaret next—only lawyer I ever liked. A will comes in handy. Not a matter of if, but when. You've got to face up to things. Eightieth birthday they give me eighty pair of socks, eighty marbles, eighty red licorice, eighty chocolate Kisses. Got to start planning. Found your way to Jesus yet? "I don't give free consultations." Tough as nails, Margaret. Only three hundred for the will. Gives me faith in young people. Woman hangs a shingle these days, a man comes with his hat in his hand. You know it's a woman's office with lavender walls and green plants in the corners. I'd give her all the strawberries in my greenhouse. I wonder what she thinks of me. Likes to chat, doesn't bill me for it. I come for you to do my will. They think we're done, old men, but we're never. All snow on top and fire down below. It's horrible.

Margaret, this is Lance West. I thought of some things to add. Addendums. I'm kind of pinned down right now. Hm? Oh, I believe the manifold was lying across the battery cable and run it down. Yes, that's right, mmhm. He mopped the bugs out of his face, staring up at Old Blue. "It ain't your fault, Blue."

The air burst gently on his cheek, cooled by the fan of the breaking water. *White sulfurous foam on the beach, saltwater scum like milk on their cherry mouths. Jesse Robert Bailey Rose Irene Raindrop Lance and Lyla. Six kiddies, two great grandkids and counting. Granddad's fixing the truck, he'll be up in a minute. I remember drinking milk in the war, it was only powdered milk, awful stuff. Left rings on the glass. Wednesdays we got canned milk. Ice cream, Sundays. I kept all her letters, she kept all of mine.*

There's that sound again. Stately like a Spanish dirge. The waves old women in black skirts standing and kneeling and standing again. Old Bill Monroe instrumental it reminds me of. Give me chills up the spine. Sad. Had cancer, thought he was dying. Old man when he made it. Age isn't everything. Jimmie Rodgers gone in his thirties. TB Too Bad Blues. Died with his boots on.

Lance turned his face to the roiling phosphorescent sea. *White horses shaking their tails at you. A million, million horses. You walk out in the morning, never know if you'll be back. I'm parking Old Blue. Red comes running. Down boy! Eat strawberries, put up my feet and pick a tape. Bluegrass Boys and the Foggy Mountain Boys and the Smoky Mountain Boys and the Tennessee Cut-Ups. Roy Acuff father of them all. George Bush a fan. Volume high as the ceiling. What days they had in Nashville. Great Speckled Bird and Mule Skinner Blues back to back at the Opry, Acuff in '38, Bill Monroe in '39. Bring down the house! I'd give anything to been in Acuff's dressing room the day Raymond Fairchild laid down his .38 and picked up his banjo. They say Loretta Lynn was singing Sweet Thing in front and backstage Roy and Bill and Archie Campbell and ten others was rubbing their jaws hearing Ray Fairchild the first time doing banjo breaks on a smoking five-string.*

But if I could go back once, just once, I'd eat Ma's bread again and roll sweet cream down my tongue and pet Sally like the first times before anybody left home before the war before the children—just holding each other while the wind howls over the plains. If I could have one wish, just one wish to make good on, I'd choose one of the old-time hymns to be a part of, we're all together finally and all's forgiven, only that ain't going backwards in time, I suppose it's going forwards, unless we're somehow souls before we're born. It's hard to say. I never did much looking back. "It's always straight ahead with you, Lance, up at dawn and face front in the saddle, off to work and never a word to spare." Much better to talk it to death, fight it over and over like a Civil War buff. You're planing wood in the shop and no preamble or nothing she marches in wringing the dishtowel in her hand, reminds you of something you said six years ago, wants to fight about it—just to see you care.

It's true, though, if you don't look back, you might not see you dropped something. Open your eyes, the kids are growed up. Red, he dogs me, I should have pet him this morning. "I ain't got time to pet you, boy." Oh I got time. I got time now. Big kiss on the nose. Put on the music. Rose Maddox! Swingingest Swing Low I ever heard. She'd turn a haunted house into a barn dance. Louder! Strobe light flashes when the phone rings. It's my lawyer. Got your message, Lance. Glad you're safe. Oh, just drinking my first cup of coffee in sixty-three years. Like to come over for some strawberries? Take me in your lifeboat? Strawberries and cream, why not? Been a long time since I was starving. Home from school I eat soda crackers or bread with butter and sugar, it tide me over till supper. There was a cold water stock well hundred thirty foot deep that was awful tasting stuff that Ma put the butter in to keep it. Sweetest bread in Sioux Falls.

All the while, the ocean trundled closer, and he heard, among the lunge and parry, the plash and wash of the sea, the rhythm of his breathing, his heart-fed pulse playing its intimate call and response

up...down
up dedown down
up deedee downdown
up deedeedown

dum deedumdum
dum deedeedumdum
da deedeedadah
da deedeeday

da-da-dah deedah
da-da-dah deeday
da-da-dah deedah deedah deedeedah

dadarumdeeda dadarumdeeday
dadaroom dadaray dadaroomdeedoomdee
rum doodarootle deedarootleetlelay
dadarootleetleaddleiddleallaiddleday—

Don Reno one of the best banjo pickers ever. Earl Scruggs passed him the break. Dead and gone. Dead and gone. I wonder who gets my miniatures. Mandolin guitar acoustic bass. Margaret liked them. Give 'em to her. Why not? It's not who gets them, it's who likes them. My tools? Router shaper welders lathes metal wood joiner radial arm table three bandsaws taps dies. "Generally it's the next of kin, but I can draw up anything you want, Lance." Where there's a will there's a way.

Old-time blacksmith sends his son to machine school to make something of him. "You should see all the things they got in machine school, Pa. They got a thing called a micrometer like a C-clamp only it measures tiny tiny things in thousandths of an inch." "Really, son? And how many thousandths are there in an inch, son?" "Oh, millions, Pa!"

Not young people's idea of a joke, I guess. Margaret laughed. Boyfriend only grunted. She's sweet. Respect her elders. Wouldn't want to marry her. Tried it twice. On the other hand. Let me take you clamming, Margaret. Sure, bring your boyfriend. Never done it? We'll cook fritters. Big smile on her face. Couldn't carve a bigger smile on a pumpkin. Bright eyes, bright lips. I always loved brown hair. Long nutty hair on a woman kills me. I'm a hundred thirty-seven when she's eighty-three. Where there's a will there's a way. Transplanted city gal. Frisco. Not exactly well educated. Recognized Willie Nelson—heard of Merle Haggard—didn't know Patsy Cline from Hillary Clinton. Never heard of Patsy! But she's interested. I like that. It ain't the knowing, it's the curiosity. Would you like to see my signed pictures? Here's Mac Wiseman and Chubby Wise and Raymond Fairchild, Little Roy Lewis and Curly Seckler and Rose Maddox and her band. Yep, this is my shrine. Sit down, I'll put on Patsy. Strawberries plump red heart-shaped: have some. Myself, no, not much of a musician myself, I sang a little tenor, carried a harmonica, but look, I've got hundreds of festival tapes they let me plug direct into the soundboard to make, video, audio. It's my love affair. The only one that's lasted. One of life's sweet spots. And the sweetness? "It's usually the next of kin, but we can write it any which way." Bah. She might be here tomorrow, she might float away. I'll drain and change the gear

*oil, repack the hub bearings, brakes. You'll be all right,
Old Blue. Long as the engine stays dry, long as the water
don't get too high. You'll be all right.*

He had an idea. If the truck floated—floated but
an inch or two—he'd be free of it. Clenching his teeth,
Lance hauled up and clawed at the tire but he hadn't
the strength to stay up. You'd better, Lance. Have to.
Have to want to. Have to want to keep his head out of
the water however tired or cold or broken he was.

Chilly tendrils of air reached him ahead of the tide,
caressed his neck and forearm and retreated. He lay
back and shivered. It's cold, you fool, you won't last
ten minutes in that water. The water, the water. He
noticed its gentle appearance; averted his eyes; then
stared good and hard at the pale shifting surf and
arched back in horror from it, the white lacework hem
of a vast gown sweeping hither and yon in the busyness
of time.

Distantly then a surprising sound. It calmed him
by compelling his attention. It even stirred him to pity,
until he recognized the screaming as his own. Such
a hue and cry! No lifeboat? No lovers on the beach?
Turning his face in the sand, thrashing from side to
side, Lance sobbed for help until there was no cry left
in him but a few hoarse coughs that sputtered out.

Tiny airborne droplets pelted him like the nibs of
unseen birds. *They come to feast on the treacle of a dead
man. To nibble at the sweet spots. Sweet? They gather on
him like the sugar spots on a fruit, all brown and creeping across him until. Stop it. Creeping across him until
he's black and. Stop it, stop it. Black and putrid and all*

soft and slimy and. Shut up, shut up! Buried under the rhubarb, fish guts, clam juice, wormy and reeking: Red dig me up.

Oh shut your mumbler. Look where she is. Everything got its season. Strawberries plump and juicy. You'd think she was a woman rustling her skirts in the dark. Little cold for starters, but she'll warm you up. Louder! Call louder! Come here, little ones. Granddad chisels on a anvil, he cuts and threads his own bolts. He follows the festivals, the stock cars, the spring races. He knows your moms and dads, he loved your grandmoms. Everyone's got a notion of when and where and what and why. Some say it's the slack tides, when your line sinks and the fish hunt the deep. Some say it's the currents, the strong tides that move the fish across your bait. If the fish are running, they're running, and if they ain't, they ain't. Get past the hokum, there's a whole world of sweetness underneath. You can't eat it or hoard it or trade your favorite toy for it. You live it. The leg I don't need. Hell, I'll shimmy on one. I've seen singers with steel jaws, the bone gone to cancer—they can't eat, but they can sing. I've seen fiddlers with hands lost to cornpickers, sawmills—they bind their bow ends to their stumps and play. They play. Rose Maddox came from sharecroppers that hopped a freight train west, she was seven years old. Jimmie Rodgers dragged a cot to his last recording, he laid him down between takes, he was hemorrhaging inside. He yodeled while he died. Go out to her, make her yours—carry her in your canoe. Put up the volume, high as the ceiling. Roy's dead but you can't keep him down. Can't run, you can't hide either. Bill Monroe in '96, Rose

Maddox just last year. But the Bashful Brother Oswald's still at it—sixty years on the Grand Ole Opry! Can't stop the band. They're all here. Ray Fairchild and the Crowe boys and the Lewis Family with Little Roy Lewis. Go on, take it. Oooh that's chill. Man and his truck, woman in a boat. Float her to the sandbar. This is my sea chariot. We dug razor clams by the bucketfuls. Clam juice running down her hands. Lips smiling. Oh lord I'd give my leg, lay down my soul for a taste of that. Tide and wind come up. Canoe's so heavy, an inch of freeboard is all we got between us and the sea, the bow's weathercocking in the wind, her hair's awhirling round her face, torrents of it, splashing like handfuls of seed, a big smile on her mouth, no fear, no fear at all. Everything glows. July already: the year's half done and I hardly know what happened to it. Oh those mornings, those mornings cut fresh off the heel of time and still dripping butter.

A Note on the Author

An award-winning novelist and essayist, Tanyo Ravicz is originally from California. After attending Harvard University, he settled for many years in Alaska, a place which continues to inspire his work. His books include *A Man of His Village* and *Ring of Fire*. Visit his website at www.tanyo.net.